PENGUIN CRIME FICTION

A CHILL RAIN IN JANUARY

L. R. Wright is the author of five previous novels, including the Edgar Award winner for 1986, *The Suspect*, and its sequel *Sleep While I Sing*, both published by Penguin.

A
CHILL
RAIN
IN
JANUARY

L. R. Wright

PENGUIN BOOKS

PENGUIN BOOKS
Published by the Penguin Group
Viking Penguin, a division of Penguin Books USA Inc.,
375 Hudson Street, New York, New York 10014, U.S.A.
Penguin Books Ltd, 27 Wrights Lane, London W8 5TZ, England
Penguin Books Australia Ltd, Ringwood, Victoria, Australia
Penguin Books Canada Ltd, 2801 John Street,
Markham, Ontario, Canada L3R 1B4
Penguin Books (N.Z.) Ltd, 182–190 Wairau Road,
Auckland 10, New Zealand

Penguin Books Ltd, Registered Offices:
Harmondsworth, Middlesex, England

First published in the United States of America by
Viking Penguin, a division of Penguin Books USA Inc., 1990
Published in Penguin Books 1991

1 3 5 7 9 10 8 6 4 2

LIBRARY OF CONGRESS CATALOGING IN PUBLICATION DATA
Wright, Laurali, 1939–
A chill rain in January/L. R. Wright.
p. cm. — (Penguin crime fiction)
ISBN 0 14 01.2982 0
I. Title.
PR9199.3.W68C47 1991
813'.54—dc20 90–19971

Printed in the United States of America

THIS BOOK
IS FOR MARY ELDRED,
AND FOR MARTI WRIGHT

ACKNOWLEDGMENTS

The author wishes to acknowledge the advice and information provided by Staff Sergeant Don Rowett, Royal Canadian Mounted Police, and by Elaine Ferbey; any inaccuracies are her own.

This book owes much to the discernment, the patience, and the generosity of John Wright.

A
CHILL
RAIN
IN
JANUARY

CHAPTER

1

Zoe's world was a dangerous place.

It made her very angry, sometimes, to think about how dangerous a place it was.

Sometimes she got so mad she didn't care what happened, and then she did things she wasn't ever supposed to do.

But she wasn't mad now, she was humming to herself, warm in her bed, snuggled into the mattress with the covers pulled up high upon her shoulders: she liked to feel like a turtle when she was in bed.

She lay on her side, facing the window. The blind was pulled down, so the world couldn't peer in at her while she slept.

Zoe lay in her bed waiting to decide to go to sleep, lay on her side, knees up, hands tucked into her chest right where she'd have breasts someday. She tried to imagine it, how it would feel to have her hands right there in the same place, but between two big breasts. "Yuck," she said to herself. But maybe she wouldn't have big ones.

Her new radio sat on the bookcase. It was a birthday present from her parents. Now she could listen to "The Green Hornet" and "Mr.

Keen" and "The Shadow" and "Inner Sanctum" even though they came on past her bedtime.

From Benjamin she'd gotten a book, and that irritated her because Benjamin knew that Zoe didn't like to read. It was like having somebody talk right into her ear or stare into her head. As soon as she opened a book she could hear the breathing of the person who wrote it.

Zoe moved her hands down there between her thighs where it was nice and warm. She let her eyes close and there was a little gentle dropping down feeling in the middle of her, and her mind started to fly away, her mind flew away to make a dream for her. Any minute now it would rush back and fill up her closed eyes with a dream. She waited, listening to her lungs breathe, waited for a dream.

Away, far away, she heard tiny sounds; dream music coming, maybe; and there was a shift in the thickness of the air; a brushing against her cheek, a pressure there, light, then heavier . . . she tried to open her eyes in the dream and couldn't and then they were open but she couldn't see anything. She moved her head and it felt sluggish and black where she was . . .

. . . like when she'd fallen into Cultus Lake and there wasn't any bottom: she'd thrashed around and fought the water until it tossed her back into the air and she yelled "Help!" feeling really stupid, but nobody paid any attention and the water sucked her down again. She beat against it with fists and feet but it moved out of reach and then back again and finally it tossed her away again and she yelled "Help!" again, and a man grabbed her under the arms and lifted her onto the jetty that stuck out into the lake. She scrambled to her feet and ran down the jetty and across the sand to where Benjamin and her parents were sitting under a tree with the picnic. She told them what had happened but she saw in their faces that they didn't believe her . . . .

Now she moved around restlessly in the blackness of her

dream—except for her head, she couldn't move her head. Her breaths sounded different, faster; and something in her chest hurt and was making her not get enough air. She opened her mouth to get more but her mouth felt squashed—something was leaning against it so she couldn't open it properly. She tried to touch her face with her hands but she only could get the pillow in her fingers.

Her heart was beating so fast it seemed to be moving around in her chest. She heard herself making noises and tried to make them louder so somebody would hear her. She lashed out with all of her body and felt her fists hit something soft that went flying and suddenly the thing leaning on her face was gone.

Zoe shoved herself onto her hands and knees and gulped and gasped until there was enough air in her lungs. Her pillow lay on the floor beside the bed. Could the pillow have done that to her, nearly smothered her to death? She looked over her shoulder at the door to the hall. It was closed. But it seemed to Zoe that the door was shuddering a little bit. As if somebody had opened it and gone through into the hall and closed it again.

Maybe somebody was after her.

She sat in bed with the covers pulled up over her shoulders. Her heart was still beating really really fast but not as fast as before, so she knew it would be all right. Her chest didn't hurt anymore.

She sat staring at the door for a long time. She wondered who could have tried to do that to her. Most likely it was Benjamin, she thought. But maybe it was her mother. Or even her father. It could have been anybody, she thought, getting very very mad about it.

She'd have to figure out a way to lock her door. So as to keep herself safe.

CHAPTER
2

Winter isn't really winter, on the Sunshine Coast.

It is not unusual to have no snow at all, and some years there is hardly any frost.

There is a lot of rain, though; and there are days of fog, too, thick and cool and wet, when the clouds descend and spread across the earth, touching the earth's face with cool, wet fingers. Karl Alberg is not greatly affected by weather, but he does notice the fog when it drifts and swirls in front of his white Oldsmobile. He doesn't like it much. He slows down, grits his teeth, and waits for it to disperse. There are days when it doesn't disperse. Then he finds himself breathing more shallowly when he's outdoors, as though afraid he will breathe in the fog and discover too late that it has substance, like cotton wool. But usually the fog does lift, around noon; it lifts, and soars up, and vanishes, in a bright brilliant sparkle of sun.

More often than fog, there is rain. Sometimes it falls steadily, heavily. Sometimes there is an apparently perpetual drizzle. In Vancouver, an hour and a half away by road and ferry, it is difficult to find a color other than gray, when the winter rain is falling. But on the Sunshine Coast, things are different.

In the woods behind Cassandra Mitchell's house there are cedar and pine trees, gray-green, sleek with raindrops. Ferns continue to grow there throughout the winter, and the salal rustles. In her backyard the branches of the holly trees are heavy with clusters of red berries, and a winter jasmine blooms yellow. Cassandra Mitchell sees the golden manes of the willow trees, and watches for the sweep of sap that reddens the pliant skeletons of blueberry bushes. She likes the gray of sea and sky; on the stillest of days there is a tremor of silver upon the sea. And the skies are constantly changing, moving, sweeping away gray to offer a clean smooth patch of cream, like a canvas stretched and ready; pools of adolescent blue, light and clear and shallow; pale shades of violet; bruisy ocher.

Ramona Orlitzki doesn't mind the fog, or the rain, either, but she often has trouble keeping herself warm, in wintertime. In her little house she used to sit in front of a heater, knitting vigorously, admiring the big waves thrown toward her garden by the sea. Now keeping her warm is somebody else's responsibility, and she can't see the ocean anymore from where she lives.

Zoe Strachan is wary of fog, and avoids it.

She tolerates the rain.

She doesn't notice holly, or willow trees, or jasmine. She sometimes sits on the rocky beach behind her house and listens to the sea, and watches it.

Zoe Strachan sees that in winter the light is different, the air is less dense.

She understands that it is winter s task each year to nurture death, and establish tranquillity.

C H A P T E R

3

One morning in late January, a gloomy, drizzly day, lightless and sullen, Zoe Strachan opened her door and stared into the face of her brother.

"Good God," she said, appalled.

He laughed, but she could see that he was nervous.

When her doorbell rang, she had as usual thought first about her car: was it parked in the driveway or hidden away in the garage? When it was in the garage she often didn't bother answering the door. But today she'd left it out.

It would be a salesman, she had thought, going reluctantly to the door. Probably real estate. Those people were always trying to get her to sell off part of her property.

Or else some child peddling raffle tickets or dried-out cookies or grizzled chocolate bars. "I don't gamble," she always said to them, or, "I don't eat sweets," or, if it was some adult person collecting for a charity, Zoe would say very firmly, "I don't give any of my money away to anyone."

But it was her brother standing there.

"I haven't heard from you in years," said Zoe.

"I know." Benjamin was tall and gaunt and somewhat stooped, and his hair was almost completely gray, even though he was only fifty-two, four years older than she.

"Where's your wife?" she said, looking behind him.

"Well, she died, I'm afraid." He wore a dark-blue suit that didn't look quite right on him.

"Died? When? Of what?"

"Cancer. Five years ago."

"That's too bad," said Zoe, formally.

"Yes," said Benjamin vaguely, looking past her into the house. "I miss her."

She ushered him in and closed the door. They stood in the small foyer for a moment and Zoe studied her brother critically. "What are you doing here? And please don't tell me you're after money again."

Benjamin appeared to wince. "Zoe," he began.

She shook her head, amazed. "The answer is no, of course."

He sighed. "At least give me lunch, or something, before you send me on my way." As he stepped through the doorway and past her, she thought she smelled alcohol.

Zoe led the way into the living room. "It's too early for lunch. I'll make some coffee." She told him to sit down, and went into the kitchen.

While the coffee brewed she rested her hands on the countertop and drummed her fingers, first the right hand, then the left, until she had done each hand five times.

He'd had plenty of money of his own, once. She didn't have the faintest idea what he'd done with it. There wasn't a frugal bone in his body, she thought, watching the water drip through the coffee into the carafe.

"Can I have an ashtray?" he said, coming into the kitchen.

"I don't smoke, Benjamin." Zoe put a mug and cream and sugar on a tray. "I don't have any ashtrays." ˙

He reached around her and got a dessert bowl from the cupboard. She watched with distaste as he flicked ashes into it, and onto the sleeve of his suit jacket, as well.

As he brushed at his sleeve she realized what was wrong with the suit. It was several sizes too large for him. She looked at him keenly, saw his pallor, and wondered if his wife could have passed her cancer on to him before she died.

"How about a little brandy," said Benjamin, "to go with the coffee."

"No." Zoe poured coffee into the mug and carried the tray into the living room. "You've got about fifteen minutes," she said, handing him the coffee, "until you have to leave to catch the next ferry."

Benjamin sat in the black leather chair that was Zoe's favorite. "You're looking very well, Zoe," he said.

"Drink your coffee."

"Every time I see you it surprises me, how well you look." He put the mug on a side table and leaned forward, arms resting on his thighs, letting his hands dangle. He had always had very unattractive hands, thought Zoe with repugnance. They had had an odd smell to them, too, when he was a boy. Sweat, probably. He had sweated a lot, when he was a boy.

"I take care of myself," she said. "That's why I look well."

"Yes. That's right. I know."

"Drink your coffee," Zoe said again.

Benjamin gazed around the living room. "It's a funny kind of place you live in."

Zoe watched him, smiling a little, but wary. He'd always been secretive. So was she, of course. But Benjamin was also unpredictable, because he had absolutely no self-discipline.

"You like it here, don't you? In this funny little house, huddled against the rocks in this funny little town."

"If I didn't like it, Benjamin," she said, "I wouldn't be here."

"It must be nice to know exactly what you want," said Benjamin.

His face, she noticed, was barren. She had been expecting grievousness, or guile, but there was nothing there at all. She began to relax. Perhaps she wouldn't have to battle with him. Perhaps one more resolute "no" would do it.

"And to be able to afford to get it," he went on. "That must be nice. And of course to keep it. That's nicer still."

"It is, yes," said Zoe. She began thinking about what she might like to have for lunch.

Benjamin sat back and picked up his coffee mug. He folded one leg over the other. "It's very serious business that's brought me here, Zoe," he said.

She waited.

"Aren't you even curious?" said Benjamin, and he sighed and shook his head when she didn't respond. "I forget, you know, how eccentric you are."

She turned her head slightly, so that she was facing him dead on, and looked straight into his eyes. He faltered, then.

"I'm afraid you have to leave now, Benjamin."

He looked at her again, so bleak and defiant that she felt a trickle of apprehension.

"Right now," she said. "Or you won't catch the next ferry."

Benjamin looked out the big window at the stone-floored patio. "Oh my dear," he said dully. "I can't catch the next ferry. We have far too much to talk about."

"We have nothing to talk about," said Zoe.

Suddenly she thought of her father. This happened

sometimes: a strange, ephemeral compassion for one of her parents flickered through her brain, alien and superfluous.

"'Shoes and ships and sealing wax . . . ,'" Benjamin intoned. He put his head back and closed his eyes. "Death," he said. "And diaries. That's what we've got to talk about." He opened his eyes and looked at her. "And yes, Zoe, you're right. Money, of course."

CHAPTER

4

Zoe knew very early in her life that she was different. This confused her only briefly. Then, all sorts of things became clear.

She also learned early that she had to tread carefully so as not to appear to be different, if she wanted to live her life with a minimum of fuss.

She thought it unlikely that she could be the only person in the entire world who was different; but she was the only person she knew who was.

Eventually Zoe created an outside person; otherwise she would have been in trouble all the time.

She made up rules for this person, and then she felt a lot safer. When she got into trouble, she knew it was because she'd broken one of the rules.

Before the creation of her outside person, it seemed to Zoe that she couldn't say or do very much at all without getting somebody annoyed. Or worse.

It made her tired and worried, in the early part of her life, to realize that everybody else lived in a different way than she did. She decided she had to understand this difference somehow.

She learned to do it by writing things down.

The first time was for school. In grade three, her class was told to write about what they'd done during their holidays. Zoe put it off and put it off, not wanting to do it, not even knowing how to do it. But every day her teacher hadn't forgotten about it. Every day she asked Zoe for her holiday story. Finally in exasperation Zoe asked her mother to help her.

They sat down together after dinner. Zoe had some paper and a pencil. Her mother said, "Tell me something you did in your holidays that you really enjoyed a lot."

Zoe thought about that. She'd enjoyed sneaking into the basement of the Nelsons' house, next door, and poking around in an old trunk she'd found there. After a minute she shrugged her shoulders.

"What about when we went on the train to Banff?" said her mother.

"I liked it in the pool," said Zoe, remembering. "Because the water was hot but the air was cool."

"You could write about that, then."

"That isn't much to say," said Zoe doubtfully.

"I don't think Miss Warren wants you to say a whole lot. Maybe enough to fill up a page. You could write about the train ride and then about the hot springs."

"What would I say about the train ride?"

"What do you remember about it?"

Zoe imagined herself putting her thoughts through a sieve. "I remember looking out the window at night," she said. "Sometimes I couldn't see any lights anywhere. I thought all the bulbs in the world had got burned out at the same time." She glanced at her mother, and saw that she was smiling.

"There, you see?" said Zoe's mother. "You have lots of things to write about."

Zoe wrote those things and Miss Warren said what she had written was very good.

Zoe thought hard about this for a long time.

She decided that it was okay if she showed other people little tiny bits of what she thought and felt about things. But that it was really important to pick the right bits.

She started writing down things for herself. First just on loose pieces of paper; trying things out.

For example: Was it all right to say the things she thought about Benjamin? she wondered on the paper.

Then she said them, to her mother.

Her mother became very upset and scolded her in a piercing voice and rushed from the room.

Zoe then said the same things to her father. For a minute his face looked as if it was caving in. Then he leaned forward until his arms were resting on his knees and he was staring at the rug.

"It's perfectly normal," he said, "to get angry with your brother. He gets angry with you sometimes, too."

He said a lot of other stuff, too, but Zoe wasn't listening anymore. There were many things that people didn't like to hear. When you said them they might pretend you didn't mean them, or they might try to persuade you not to mean them anymore, or they might just get mad. Either it was very boring or, if you got them mad, you could get yelled at, or slapped.

Eventually Zoe used her allowance to buy herself a scribbler, a notebook, where she could say things other people wouldn't want to hear. And gradually, with the help of the scribbler, she got things sorted out.

When she was little and had seen something she wanted very badly she had always just taken it, even when it belonged to *somebody else. But this led to uproar and punishment. So she made a rule about it: "Don't steal anything unless you can be sure nobody's going to find out who did it."*

When people asked her questions, she was in the habit of saying whatever came into her head. A lot of times these were made-up things. This got her into trouble, too. So she wrote in the exercise book: "Don't say anything about anything unless you have to, and then try to say just a little bit, and make at least some of it true."

When something made her angry she struck out at it, whether it was a person or a thing, because this used up the anger. She disliked being angry. It was a hot, tight feeling which was very uncomfortable. But hitting, it seemed, was even worse than stealing; especially when she broke things. So one of her rules said: "When you get angry go away where nobody can see you and hit things that won't break. And if your angriness still won't go away, figure out a way to get back at the person you're angry with so that nobody knows you did anything to her. Or him."

She made up an outside Zoe who was able to live by these rules. This was Zoe Number Two.

Zoe Number One lived safe inside her head, and came out only when she was alone, and spoke aloud only in the scribblers.

CHAPTER

5

"There's a car parked out by the Strachan woman's place," said Sandy McAllister, tossing the day's mail on the counter. He was a small, wiry man of about forty who wore the postal worker's summer uniform of shorts and knee socks all year round. Today he had also donned the winter cape, hooded and waterproof.

"So what?" said Isabella Harbud from her desk.

"Took her some mail today." He leaned over the counter, to watch Isabella type.

"That's your job, isn't it?"

"You're sure fast on that thing," he said admiringly, scratching the back of his calf with the front of his other foot. "She's one of the few people in town, most days they don't get any. Makes you wonder."

"You ought to mind your own business, Mr. Sandy McAllister, that's what you ought to do." She whipped the paper from her typewriter and scrutinized it critically.

"Nice car it is, too. Not many people visit that one, I'll tell you," said Sandy, hoisting the mailbag farther onto his shoulder.

"You stop your gossip and get on about your business," said Isabella. She slapped the letter on top of a pile of completed correspondence and cranked another sheet of paper into the typewriter.

Sandy shrugged, hurt. "I'm just trying to make conversation. You got time for a coffee?"

Isabella shot him a disapproving look. "Of course I don't. What would my hubby think, if I were to go off for a coffee with the likes of you?"

"Hoo hoo hoo, he'd be plenty worried, all right." He gave her a wink and headed for the door.

A small, furtive-looking woman darted into the reception area from the hall. She shook her head vigorously at Isabella and rushed outside, one step ahead of the mailman. Isabella looked after her and sighed. She glanced doubtfully over the counter at the woman who sat in the waiting area. "You're next," she said, getting to her feet.

Staff Sergeant Karl Alberg of the Sechelt detachment, Royal Canadian Mounted Police, studied a list that lay upon the desk in front of him. He picked up a pencil and laboriously stroked through the first name that appeared on it. "Come," he said when Isabella knocked on the door. She ushered the candidate in without looking at Alberg, and left quickly.

Alberg stared at the woman who had planted herself firmly in the middle of his office. She stood five feet one inch tall, weighed over two hundred pounds, and had very little hair.

"So," he said finally, glancing down at his list. "Mrs.— Stratidakis, is it?"

"It's a good Greek name."

"Greek, yes, that's what I thought it was. Tell me about yourself, Mrs. Stratidakis."

"I brought up eight kids, looked after all their wants, and my man's, too." Her small black eyes darted uneasily around the office. "I've never been in a police station before in my life. I'm a decent woman."

"Do you do any cooking? Or just cleaning?"

"I do it for none, now, but my man and me. And I would do no cooking, no, sir." Alberg noticed that the small amount of hair she possessed clung to her scalp in sparse outcroppings that looked rather like feathers. "And I would charge you considerable," she said darkly, "for coming in here every day, to this police station."

"It's not my office I want cleaned," said Alberg. "It's my house. In Gibsons." Gibsons Landing is a town about twenty miles south of Sechelt.

She gazed at him curiously. "You got no wife, huh?" She was perspiring a lot.

"I'm divorced," said Alberg. Her face clouded instantly with suspicion. "Oh, well," said Alberg to himself. He stood up. "I don't need to keep you any longer, Mrs. Stratidakis. Thank you for coming. Isabella will be in touch with you."

He closed the door after her, counted to thirty, opened it, and thundered, "Isabella!" When she appeared he said, "What the hell happened to that woman's head?"

"I hadn't met her myself," said Isabella. "She'd be a good hard worker, I'm told."

"She doesn't like police officers," he said sullenly. "She doesn't approve of divorced men."

"My hubby gave me her name. He treated her son." Isabella's husband was a chiropractor.

"Promise me, Isabella, that you won't usher in another

single damn candidate unless you've seen her first with your own beautiful golden eyes." He crumpled the list and tossed it in the wastepaper basket.

"You can trust me," she said. Then, solemnly, she handed him a telephone message. She thrust some wayward strands of long auburn hair into the makeshift bun at the back of her head. "I heard she was back," she said, nodding, and eased herself out of the office.

Alberg picked up the phone and dialed the library.

"You're back," he said, when Cassandra Mitchell answered. "Jesus. Finally."

"How are you, Karl?"

"A whole lot better than I was a couple of minutes ago. How was England?"

"Great. Terrific. But I'm glad to be home. It feels like I've been gone for years."

"You have. Years." Actually she'd been away only four months, but it had felt like years to Alberg. "When am I going to see you?" She sounded incredibly sexy, over the phone. "How about tonight?"

"I have to see my mother tonight. But I wondered, do you want to have lunch?"

His office door opened and Isabella stood there, white-faced, wringing her hands.

"Yeah. Lunch. That's great."

"Karl," said Isabella. She never called him Karl.

"I have to go, Cassandra. I'll see you at noon," said Alberg, and hung up.

"What is it?" He went to her quickly, thinking about car crashes, and Isabella's seventeen-year-old son.

But it wasn't Isabella's son.

It was Ramona Orlitzki.

CHAPTER
6

There was no facility in Sechelt designed to look after elderly people incapable of caring for themselves. So they were housed on the top floor of the hospital. And that's where Ramona Orlitzki ended up.

Ramona was in her mid-seventies, tall and thin, with scrimpy hair and quick hands.

Her husband, whose name was Anton, had died in 1980, and for several years after that Ramona lived happily by herself in a cottage next to the sea. The cottage was too cold in the worst days of winter, but there weren't many of those, and she had a good, reliable heater.

Ramona read voraciously. She particularly liked books with a lot of robust, juicy sex in them and would ask Cassandra Mitchell, the librarian, to keep her eye peeled for the kind of thing Ramona would enjoy.

She was fond of saying, when her health was inquired after, that at her age she could expect anything but pregnancy; and then she'd laugh, squeezing up her face and wheezing, producing no actual laughter, just a lot of wheezing, and people watched, smiling but tense, and were relieved when Ramona recovered, wiped her eyes, and winked. She wore many layers of clothing all the time, all year long, and in this she resembled her friend Isabella Harbud.

Ramona's husband, Anton, had been a perfectly nice man, the town was agreed upon that, but he was painfully shy, and when he and Ramona moved to Sechelt upon their retirement, he burrowed himself a refuge and with exquisite stubbornness refused to leave it, except when absolutely necessary.

Ramona had expected that retirement would bring him out of his shell, but that was clearly not to be. He never wanted to go bowling, or to a movie, or even to the restaurant on the corner for a bite to eat.

Anton said he didn't begrudge Ramona her going out and about, but she knew that deep in his heart his feelings were hurt; he had been hoping that in retirement Ramona would become more of a homebody, just as she had been hoping that he would want to go out more.

So Ramona began keeping herself at home. She loved Anton, no doubt about that; after all, she'd lived with him day in and day out for fifty years, what's that if not love, she'd say with a shrug. But she began to get pretty tired of staying in. "I'm chafing at the bit, is what I am," she confided to Isabella, and then one day Anton got sick, and zap, just like that, the poor man was gone.

And Ramona discovered that she had more friends than she'd realized; it was this discovery, rather than grief, that moved her to tears. They rallied round, her friends and neighbors. Bringing food, as people always do when there's been a death. Inviting her to stay with them until she was over it. Taking her off to church and suchlike.

For the next several years Ramona lived what she herself called a blissful life. She tended her garden, went for walks, spent time with her friends, did household chores—laundry, watering the plants, making the grocery list, paying her bills, that sort of thing.

Every week she wrote notes to her children, and every two or three months she prepared her contribution to the Family Letter that circulated among her five brothers, two sisters, and herself. She joined the Old Age Pensioners and went to bowling, and dances, and sing-songs, and on the twice-yearly bus trips to Reno. She started to have her hair done, short and curly, a perm four times a year, regular as clockwork. She discovered a fondness for gin. She worked a little bit at the library, for Cassandra, as a volunteer, and threw the fear of God into careless people who thought only of themselves and never could be bothered returning books on time. She had lunch every Wednesday with Isabella and went out clamming from time to time with her friend Rosie, who lived four doors down. Every year in the summertime one of her children came to visit; Horace and his wife, Ella, from Cache Creek, or Martha and her husband, Jerome, who lived in Regina. And the grandchildren, two each. Ramona wasn't all that fond of the grandchildren.

Anyway, she was a fixture in the town, and her many friends and acquaintances were genuinely distressed when it turned out that there was something wrong with Ramona's innards. She had an operation, and lots of people visited her in the hospital, bringing flowers and fruit, and knowing that she liked a nip or two of an evening, they smuggled in little bottles of gin, too, the kind served on airplanes or offered for sale as stocking stuffers at Christmastime.

Eventually Ramona had recovered enough to totter on home. The Meals On Wheels people brought dinner right to her door, and other volunteers from the community took her shopping, and did her laundry, and gave her floors a sweep. But it turned out that the operation hadn't done the trick, so she had to go back and have another one, and then a third one, and by the time it was all finally over, she had, as she put it to Isabella, "about half a mile of synthetic tubing inside me and a heavy weakness upon me that just won't go away no matter how many vitamins I take."

And her mind began to wander. She knew it was wandering, too. She would start to tell Isabella something, maybe something from her Family Letter, and then she'd stop and say, "Have I already told you this?"

She liked to sit in her rocking chair, by the window in her tiny living room, where she could see the garden and, beyond it, the sea and the Trail Islands and the shallow bay that curved off to the right and the promontory at the westernmost stretch of it, where the lights of the Strachan woman's house could be seen; when Ramona sat in darkness looking out upon the night, the Strachan house looked as if it must be a boat at sea, so remote from other lights it seemed.

Sometimes Ramona would get up, pushing herself out of the rocking chair and hanging on to the easy chair that sat next to it—that was where Anton had liked to sit, thumbing through the newspaper and looking out from time to time at the ocean and the sky. Often she'd seen him smile contentedly—she had that knowledge to comfort her, the man had died happy; she'd done her duty by him, and then she'd gotten to enjoy life, too; she'd galloped through the next few years with the fervor of a filly, God help her, it was true . . .

And now look where she'd ended up, hauling herself out of her chair and into the kitchen, then looking around, wondering what in the world she was doing there.

Strange things happened. One time, for instance, she didn't recognize the wallpaper in the bedroom: "Did I just put that up, then?" she said to herself, and she went close to the wall to have a look-see, but no, the paper was worn and faded here and there, and when she pulled a picture away from the wall and peered in behind it the paper was much brighter in there, where light hadn't been able to get at it.

Then of course she couldn't remember why on earth she was inspecting the wallpaper so intently.

A big circle, she swept slowly around in a great big circle, couldn't get out of it, it kept changing, looking different, but it was the same circle, she knew it.

In the evenings she sat quietly in the rocking chair and looked out the window or watched television and sipped her gin. The television usually made sense to her, and as time passed, it became more comforting company than real people; it stayed pretty much the same from day to day, but not entirely completely the same, so that if it looked familiar, that was good and if sometimes she didn't recognize something, that was all right, too; it didn't necessarily mean she'd forgotten anything. But real people—they often looked at her pityingly now, and she felt the heat of humiliation sweep up her neck and across her face and she felt exposed and vulnerable and then she got snappish. When visitors left she was relieved but very depressed, too. She knew she'd been rude, she hadn't been able to help it, and she felt terrible about it.

Finally her doctor, who was Alex Gillingham, came to her house and talked to her like a Dutch uncle.

"You've got to come and live in the hospital," he told her, straight out. "There's lots to do there," he said. "Maybe you can teach some of the other people there how to knit. You can go out in the garden. You can go to the library when you feel like it. Dammit, Ramona, the place isn't a jail."

Well, she told Isabella, he went on and on like that, ranting and raving, and really, she didn't have any choice. And maybe, secretly, maybe she was even a little bit relieved, at first. There were some things that scared her; like forgetting to turn off the stove.

When she had to write it in the Family Letter she started to cry, telling her brothers and sisters what was happening to her. Tears got all over the page—and that brought her up short; she crumpled that piece of paper and started all over again and tried to put a better face on the situation than it deserved. There wasn't any point in worrying them; they were too far away to do anything useful.

She wrote her children, too, although she knew they wouldn't be surprised to get the news. They'd been clucking over her for a couple of years now, wanting her to move into the hospital. She'd certainly noticed, she certainly wasn't that far gone, that neither of them had said a single word about whether she might want to go and live with them. But she wouldn't have wanted to go to Cache Creek or Regina anyway; colder than Siberia it was in both those places, and she didn't know a soul in either one except her lugubrious children.

Horace said he guessed she'd be selling the house now, but Ramona was having none of that.

"It could be just a temporary stay," she said firmly, "it could be I'll be back there in a jiffy; meanwhile I'm going to rent it out," and she did.

For a while, after she moved into the hospital, her friends thought Ramona had rallied.

Isabella went often to visit her, and so did Rosie, and Cassandra stopped by before she left for England, and they all went away feeling relieved. Ramona seemed brighter, more confident, more like her old self.

Several months passed.

And then Ramona began complaining to Dr. Gillingham about the treatment she was getting. Nobody was ever available when she wanted to be taken someplace, she said. She hadn't had a perm in six months, she looked terrible, and there wasn't anybody to take her to the hairdresser.

"What are you talking about? You've got all sorts of friends to take you places," said the doctor.

"I've got no right burdening my friends with things like that," said Ramona angrily. "It's one of the nurses ought to take me." He tried to reason with her, but she waved her hands in his face, shooing away his words. "That's what they're here for," she insisted.

And she had other complaints, as well. Her room looked out over the roof of the adjoining wing; she didn't have a view. It was too cold outside to garden, or walk, and besides, those stupid nurses wouldn't let her out without they put her in a damn wheelchair, if you can believe that. "And on top of it all," she concluded bitterly, "they won't let me have my gin here."

This, it seemed, was the crux of it.

The nurses remained obdurate. Ramona wasn't to have her gin.

It's hard to know how much the one thing had to do with the other, but it is true that the nurse who came to summon her for breakfast on that Wednesday morning in January found Ramona's bed empty, and Ramona gone.

C H A P T E R

7

Benjamin had had the temerity only once before to appear uninvited at Zoe's front door.

The other time had been on a summer day more than seven years earlier. Zoe had just moved into her house. She hadn't gotten to know the place yet; she hadn't arranged the furniture or set up her workroom. She'd even been beset by doubts that she'd made the right decision, buying the property, having the house built. On the day that Benjamin came, she was unpacking boxes in the kitchen, scolding herself, telling herself to have the strength of her convictions, reminding herself that if for whatever reason it didn't work out, she could always move.

Oh, but she did not want to move. Not again.

Both sets of French doors were open wide to the patio, and the front door was open, too, allowing the summer breezes to sweep through and make the whole house cool. Zoe was wearing shorts and a T-shirt and sneakers.

She had driven into Sechelt, to the supermarket in the little mall, first thing in the morning to buy a pail, some Mr. Clean, several rolls of paper towels, a couple of sponges, plain white shelf paper, and two inexpensive tea towels, which she tore in half to use as rags.

She had cleaned the countertops thoroughly, and the cupboards. They were already pretty clean, since the house was brand-new, but Zoe wiped them out and then laid the shelf paper. The fridge and stove and dishwasher were all new, too, and didn't need cleaning, but she cleaned them anyway.

Around noon she made herself a cup of tea and heated a can of soup. She sat at the kitchen table to eat lunch, and as she ate she could hear the sound of the sea coming in through the open doors and windows, and it was the only sound there was. Zoe began to feel confident again. She had her own fortress, so to speak. A solid, sturdy house out on a promontory, its face to the sea, its back to the rest of the world. It had precisely the amount of space she required: a bedroom with two closets, so she had plenty of room for what she thought of as her costumes; an office in which to do her accounts; a laundry room; and a living room; and in the basement, lots of space for a workroom and for the storage of food and supplies. In the workroom, she would refinish furniture. This was Zoe's only avocation. Restoring good pieces to their original beauty was, she had discovered, conducive to achieving tranquillity. Oh, yes, Zoe thought with satisfaction, she was going to thoroughly enjoy this house, feel thoroughly safe here, in the first brand-new, unsullied house she had ever lived in.

She finished the soup and washed out the bowl and put it

away. The rest of the soup, in a small saucepan, went into the fridge. She poured the rest of the tea into her mug, washed the pot and put it away, and prepared to open another box.

And then, seven years ago, the doorbell had rung, and she had heard Benjamin call out, "Can I come in?"

Bent over a cardboard carton, Zoe became immobile.

How had he driven over gravel up to her wide-open front door without her hearing him? She had lost her vigilance; just for a moment—but a moment was too long.

She straightened, turned, and walked out of the kitchen and down the hall to the front door.

She looked at her brother. "How did you know where I was?"

"The lawyer knows," said Benjamin. "I guess you didn't tell him it was supposed to be a secret."

"It's not supposed to be a secret. But I don't like uninvited guests. What do you want?"

He held out a bottle of wine. "Housewarming present," he said with a smile.

"I don't want you in here." Zoe raised her hand and placed it on his chest and pushed, gently. "This is my house."

Benjamin bent to put the bottle of wine on the floor just inside the door. "Okay," he said, and stood straight again. "Whatever you say." He took a couple of steps backward, away from the house. "But I need to talk to you."

She shook her head. "No. No money. You know that, Benjamin. You know I won't give you a cent. Go."

"Please, Zoe," said Benjamin quietly. "Just listen to me. I want to talk to you about Great North Mines."

Zoe looked at him with slightly more interest. "Go around to the back," she said after a minute. "There's a patio there."

She shut the door, locked it, and made her way through the

house to her bedroom. She closed the French doors there and went into her office, and stepped through another set of French doors onto the patio, closing the doors behind her.

Benjamin was looking out over the rocky windbreak at the sea.

"You want to talk about the company," said Zoe, leaning against the side of the house.

He turned to face her. "Things are beginning to go a little better for me," he said. "I kind of went to pieces when Laura divorced me."

Zoe waited.

"Lost my job, went through most of my money," Benjamin continued. "Well, you know all that. But I never sold the Great North stock," he said. "I hung on to that, no matter what."

"And now?" said Zoe dryly.

"I've gotten married again," said Benjamin.

She looked at him more closely. He had more flesh on him than he'd had the last time she saw him. His clothes were clean and pressed—summer slacks, a short-sleeved shirt. His face looked rested.

"Has she got any money?" said Zoe.

Benjamin smiled a little. "Yes," he said. "As a matter of fact, she has."

"Her own? Or family money?"

"Both," said Benjamin. "I was getting to this. I wish you wouldn't be so damn blunt." He sighed. "She inherited, but she's made it grow. She has good instincts."

"What's this got to do with Great North?"

Zoe's new patio furniture was stacked against the house. Benjamin glanced at it. "Do you mind if I get us a couple of chairs?"

"Go ahead," said Zoe.

"I've got another job, too," he said as he set up the chairs.

"Good," said Zoe.

He sat down and stretched out his legs. "I'd like to be able to give Lorraine something to invest for me," he said. "I told you, her instincts are very good. Sit down, why don't you?"

Zoe watched him, and continued to wait.

Benjamin rubbed the back of his neck. "Okay, okay. How would you like to lend me some money?" he said finally.

Zoe laughed.

"I'll give you the Great North shares as collateral." He leaned forward, earnestness slathered all over his face. "And you know what that stock means to me. But I'll be able to pay you back in no time. With interest."

"Great North's in a slump," said Zoe.

"It's just a matter of time," said Benjamin. "It's going to double in value over the next ten years."

"Then why are you willing to risk losing it?"

"It's no risk, I told you. I'll be able to repay you within months. I've seen Lorraine work. She's very shrewd, Zoe. You might want to talk to her yourself."

"I do all right on my own," said Zoe.

"So how about it?"

Zoe shook her head.

"Jesus, Zoe."

"Borrow on it from the bank."

"I can't," he said sullenly.

"Don't tell me. You've already used it as collateral."

"No I haven't," said Benjamin furiously. He got up and began pacing the patio, his hands thrust into his pockets.

"You want to borrow from me," said Zoe, "because nobody else will lend you anything no matter what collateral you come up with, because you're already in debt up to your eyebrows."

Benjamin glared at her.

"I won't give you a loan," said Zoe. "But I'll buy you out."

"I don't want to do that," said Benjamin.

"I know you don't," said Zoe. "But you will."

C H A P T E R

8

Ramona had a theory that people got a lot of second chances.

Once years and years ago she'd been driving her car, at night, when all of a sudden a great truck had roared out of a side street toward her from the left, its lights blaring. Ramona's road just happened to curve away right then, and the truck missed her—but what if I'd been there just a fraction of a second earlier? she thought, and then somehow she knew she'd lived that moment twice; the first time, she *had* been there a fraction of a second earlier, and been killed as a result, and then had yelled and complained so loudly that God decided he'd made a mistake, and he'd let her live it again and do it right this time.

Usually, though, you didn't know about your second chances, so you didn't know enough to be grateful.

That was Ramona's theory, anyway.

Tuesday night, when Mrs. Wallsten, the night nurse, arrived

with her sleeping pill, Ramona looked at it and had that same sense of having lived this moment before.

Without even thinking about why, she only pretended to gulp it down.

When Mrs. Wallsten left the room, Ramona fished the pill out from under her tongue and looked at it expectantly, as if it were now going to explain to her why it hadn't been swallowed.

She didn't sleep well, of course. Her body had gotten used to being drugged every night. Along about five o'clock Wednesday morning her bones were aching and her head felt hot and heavy. She threw back the covers and sat on the edge of the bed.

And it was then she decided to skedaddle right on out of there.

She didn't sit around thinking about it; she just got busy and did it.

Slowly, a little bit at a time, she opened the squeaky door of the metal locker that served as a closet. She got out her long-sleeved cotton housedress, a heavy cardigan, her sneakers, and her tweed coat.

From bureau drawers she selected a pair of knee-highs, two pairs of long socks, and some underwear.

Ramona dressed herself, brushed her teeth, and combed her hair. She was hurrying now.

She found a brown shopping bag in the locker and loaded into it extra underwear and socks, her toiletries, and several magazines. She kind of wished she'd planned this out in advance, so she could have laid in a stock of paperback books to take along. But she was pretty sure it was the kind of thing best done on impulse.

She buttoned up her coat, put on the white woolen gloves that were stuffed in the pocket, and wrapped around her neck the red woolen scarf that was tucked into one of the sleeves. Then she opened the door a crack and peered out into the hall.

Everything was very quiet. She couldn't see Mrs. Wallsten, who ought to have been sitting at the nurses' station in the middle of the corridor. Ramona picked up the shopping bag and eased herself out into the hall, closing the door softly behind her.

Tiptoeing, she made her way toward the nurses' station, and when she got there she saw a mug of coffee, steaming, and heard the muffled sound of a toilet flushing behind a door somewhere. She scurried past, toward the elevator, but decided when she got there to walk down.

She met nobody in the stairwell, which was bright and echoey.

When she reached the main floor, she opened the door to the lobby just a crack and saw at the switchboard a female form huddled over a book. Ramona waited there until the phone buzzed and the switchboard operator turned slightly away to answer it. Then Ramona gripped her shopping bag hard, slipped into the lobby, and scurried to the front doors, her face all screwed up in anticipation of a yell: "Hey! You! Where do you think you're going!" But there wasn't any yell, and then Ramona was out the door and into God's gray winter rain; she'd had no idea rain could ever feel so good.

It wasn't yet light, as she made her way down the hill into town.

She had a long walk ahead of her. It was about four miles, she figured, to the house.

Four miles. That would at least give her plenty of time to try to remember where she'd left the spare key.

She was exhausted, and already shivering with cold, but her spirits were so light she felt weightless.

And her mind, she knew, was sharp as a tack.

CHAPTER

9

Benjamin was part of her earliest memories. He littered her reminiscence. She saw him everywhere, a pale face with a wrinkled forehead peeking at her from around a corner, over a table, sometimes from behind their mother, whose skirt he was probably clutching.

Zoe resented him for being larger than she. And that never changed—he was always larger. He was already four when she was born, so he had a big head start, and he never lost it.

He stopped paying attention to her when she got old enough to go to school, which was a relief. But in the first part of her life he seemed to have been constantly present, hanging around and staring. The things she did always appeared to surprise him; she hated having him gawk at her all the time.

Once, when Zoe was about four and he eight, their family was visiting an aunt and uncle in Vancouver, and their mother took Zoe and Benjamin to a park across the street. They played on the swings for a while. There was nobody else around. The sun was shining, but it was a cool day.

A man had raked fallen leaves into a pile, and after a while he set fire to them and went a little way away to rake up another bunch of leaves into another pile. Benjamin went over to watch the first pile of leaves burn, and Zoe and their mother followed him.

Zoe was wearing a gray coat and a gray hat that tied under her chin, but winter rainboots weren't necessary yet, nor the leggings that matched the coat and hat. The backs of her bare legs were cool, almost cold, but the fronts of them were warm, almost hot, because of the fire. It was making a lot of crackling sounds, and she could smell the nice smell the leaves made as they burned. They floated upward in the flames, sometimes, and they were squirming or dancing, she couldn't decide which.

Her mother had her by the hand. Benjamin was apart from them, standing right next to the fire and kicking leaves into it.

"Stop it, Benjamin," said their mother. "You'll set your shoe on fire."

Benjamin thought this was very funny, and he laughed and laughed, and flung himself around in the air like a hoop going round and round, while Zoe watched him. Finally he fell down on the ground and put his hands under his head and stared up at the blue sky.

Zoe wanted to pull loose from her mother's hand, but she didn't, because if she did she'd get a startled look and maybe a frown. Her mother was staring at the fire and not paying any attention to her, and that's the way Zoe liked it.

Then she heard her mother give a little sigh. She squeezed Zoe's hand and let it go, so that she could rummage around in her handbag for a handkerchief. When she'd found it she snapped the bag shut and made little dabbing motions at her eyes, and then buried her nose in the crunched-up handkerchief and blew it. Zoe stepped away from her, just a bit, not wanting to get her germs.

She bumped into her aunt's cat, called Myrtle, which had

followed them across the street and into the park. Zoe looked down at Myrtle disapprovingly and nudged it in the ribs with the side of her foot. Myrtle gave a little squawk and then rubbed her body against Zoe's leg. "Quit that," Zoe told the cat.

"Leave Myrtle alone, Zoe," said Benjamin.

Myrtle stretched way up and dug her claws into Zoe's new gray coat.

"Quit that," said Zoe again, pushing the cat away.

"Mom," said Benjamin, "she's being mean to Myrtle."

The cat went right back to Zoe and sat at her feet, leaning against her patent-leather shoes. Zoe, exasperated, reached down and picked up the cat and tossed it into the fire.

This created a huge commotion. Benjamin scrambled to his feet and ran around and around the fire, hollering. The cat screamed and bashed around among the burning leaves and finally rolled out of the flames: it looked as if it had smoke coming out of it. It got to its feet and fled drunkenly across the park, evading Benjamin's outstretched arms, ignoring his cries of sympathy.

Zoe's mother looked as if she felt dizzy or something. She kept staring at Zoe and saying her name, over and over again, as though she couldn't believe Zoe was really standing there, as if Zoe had just suddenly appeared, out of nowhere.

The man raking leaves had straightened up to watch the cat hobbling across the park, followed by a shrieking Benjamin. He turned to look curiously at Zoe and her mother.

"What did you do?" said Zoe's mother.

"I put Myrtle in the fire."

"But why? How could you do such a terrible thing?" She was staring at Zoe and hanging on to her purse with both hands. The purse had a couple of new scratches on it—places where the leather had been made less brown. Zoe thought Myrtle had probably done that, with her stupid claws.

"*I don't know. She made me angry.*"

Her mother turned around so that her back was to Zoe, and then she turned the rest of the way around, so that she was looking straight at her again. "*Didn't you hear it screech? Don't you know how much it must hurt?*"

"*But—it wasn't me,*" *said Zoe.*

"*But you just said—you just said, I heard you, 'I put Myrtle in the fire.' You just told me that.*"

"*Yes,*" *said Zoe.* "*I mean, it wasn't me that hurt.*"

CHAPTER

10

Ramona was numb with cold, dizzy with tiredness, as she stumbled the last mile or so to her house. Her mind had gone away somewhere. It was her body that remembered the way, and her body, too, that remembered where the key was. She floundered through the gate and was about to ask herself for the fiftieth time, where did I leave that key, when all of a sudden she was bending over and scrabbling in the dirt under the big mossy rock that stood beneath the bedroom window. And there it was.

Once inside, she collapsed on the sofa and just sat there for a while, she didn't know how long, being glad she wasn't walking any longer, wishing she had a cup of coffee, looking out the living room window toward the promontory on the other side of the little bay; there weren't any lights on at the Strachan woman's house. She probably didn't get up this early.

Ramona wanted to stay there indefinitely, gathering her strength, but pretty soon she had to go to the bathroom.

And besides, she knew she had to hide herself, because they'd be trying to find her, and this house was the first place they'd think to look.

The house was cold. As soon as they'd come and gone, she'd turn on the heater.

Meanwhile, though, she'd make herself a cup of instant coffee, and she'd be sure to snatch the kettle off the burner before it started to whistle, in case the sound carried next door.

But she couldn't find her whistling kettle. There was an electric one on the counter, so she used that.

She poked around the house, looking for a good hiding place. Sometimes she stopped and rubbed her head, trying to remember why it was that she needed to hide. But she continued to feel very urgent about it, so she kept on looking, and thinking, and finally she decided on the closet. There were a lot of clothes hanging in there, and some of them went right to the floor. So she moved these out from the wall and in behind them she stacked the quilt from the double bed, and two extra blankets and a pillow that she found in the linen closet.

She was still very cold, so she took off her coat and put on three of the sweaters that hung in the closet, and struggled back into her coat, which she then couldn't get buttoned up.

Ramona settled herself in her nest to drink her coffee. And after a while, slowly, gradually, things cleared, like a wind blowing away clouds, and she remembered that Marcia and Robbie Litwin lived in her house now and that they were on a holiday somewhere, and that's why she'd decided to come here.

"Well, that's a relief," she said out loud; it was a good feeling, having a mind that was crisp and definite again.

She put it to work on the question of supplies. She had seen a few things in the freezer compartment of the fridge, and some cans in the cupboard, and she knew that out in the toolshed were boxes of potatoes and carrots and onions Marcia had grown last summer. But she ought to have fruit, and juice, and vitamins. And of course some gin; Marcia and Robbie didn't seem to have anything at all in the way of alcoholic beverages.

But she knew the neighbors to the left, the Ferrises, they liked a drink from time to time. She'd have to keep an eagle eye open, and as soon as they drove off somewhere she'd see if she could find a way in. They wouldn't begrudge her a bit of gin. They had a dog, a small one with big ears and a lot of white hair tied up on top of its head with a ribbon. She wouldn't have to worry about the dog, though, because everywhere the Ferrises went, that dog went, too.

Ramona stopped breathing, the mug of coffee halfway to her mouth. A car had stopped in front of the house, which was only about four feet from the road.

She heard the door open, and somebody got out and came lumbering around the side of the house.

My God, she thought. What did I do with my shopping bag?

C H A P T E R

11

"Okay," said Sid Sokolowski, lowering himself into the extra chair in Alberg's office. Isabella was standing by the door, clutching her elbows. "Here's the story." He picked up one foot and then the other, pulling at the pantlegs that weren't quite big enough to comfortably accommodate his huge thighs. "She's gone, all right. Not a sign of her. Those nurses are in what you might call disarray, since she isn't one of their regular escapees." The sergeant shook his head disapprovingly. "Hard to figure how those old folks can just sashay out of there without anybody noticing."

"My feelings exactly," said Isabella, nodding vigorously.

"You'd rather the place had bars?" said Alberg.

Sokolowski decided to ignore this. "Anyways, Isabella got them to file a missing persons report."

"Because I figured the sooner you get going on this, the sooner you're going to find her," said Isabella.

"Which they were willing to do," said Sokolowski patiently, "on account of like I said, she's never done this before." He looked down at his notes. "She went missing sometime between two and eight in the morning. That's as close as they can figure it."

"The night nurse makes the rounds at two," Isabella put in, "and then nobody would be looking in on her again until the shift changed at eight." She rubbed her hands. "Oh dear, oh dear. Poor Ramona."

"Is she wandering around town in a hospital gown, or what?" said Alberg.

"They wear their own clothes," said Isabella.

"Isabella. Let's hear what the sergeant has to say. Sid? What's she wearing?"

"Yeah, they wear their own clothes," said Sokolowski. "But the nurses don't know all what's supposed to be in her room, so they can't tell us what she put on. Except her coat's missing. Which is good." He licked the end of his finger and turned a page in his notebook.

"Have you been to her house?" said Isabella. "She loved that house. It's the first place she'd go."

Sokolowski looked plaintively at Alberg.

"Isabella," said Alberg. "Stop interrupting, or leave. Okay?"

"Understood," said Isabella, hugging herself.

"Yeah, she owns a house," said Sokolowski. "She's got it rented out. I went over there. The place is all shut up, nobody home. Talked to the neighbors. The tenants, they're a young couple, kinda hard up, they won some kind of drugstore contest or something, they're off to Hawaii for three weeks." He looked up from his notebook. "You notice it's always the ones on welfare enter the contests? How do you figure it, Karl?"

"Why not? They've got nothing to lose, right? Anything else?"

"Yeah, I found out it's Gillingham who's her doctor, God help the poor lady," said Sokolowski fervently. "I talked to him. Has she got any money, who are her friends, where's she likely to go—that's what I asked him. He wasn't much help, which doesn't surprise me. The guy's a flake."

"Sid."

"Yeah. Well, he doesn't know much about her finances. I've gotta go see her lawyer about that. Gillingham gave me a list of people who visit her there in the hospital. She's got two kids; he told me how to get in touch with them." He looked up again, his forehead furrowed. "Don't want to do that just yet, though, Karl. They're not locals. And she's not gonna be hard to find. Don't want to worry her kids just yet."

"Put her on the computer anyway, in case she's on her way to them. Where do they live?"

"Cache Creek and Regina," said Isabella. "She wouldn't go to them. Oh dear, oh dear," she said, wringing her hands again. "I wish she'd come to me."

"Maybe she will, Isabella," said Alberg. "But whether she does or not, we'll find her."

The sergeant nodded. "Before the day's out. I'd bet on it. Jesus, Isabella, she's an old lady, got a mind that wanders, no pennies in her jeans—we'll find her, all right."

"She won't be wearing jeans," said Isabella. "You can count on that."

"Well, whatever," said Sokolowski. "Anyway, you get my drift."

"Okay, go see her lawyer," said Alberg. "Find out if she's

got access to any cash. Isabella, are you up to helping out?"

"Well of course I am."

"Phone around to people she knew and liked, places she went to regularly. Tell them to keep their eyes open for her."

"Yes. That's a good idea. I will. Right away," said Isabella, and she left the room.

"At least it's not too bad out there," said Sokolowski, peering through the slats of the venetian blind at the gray, drizzly day. He glanced at his watch. "I better get over to the lawyer. I'll keep you posted."

When he'd left, Alberg sat there thinking about the filmmaker in Quebec who'd had Alzheimer's disease. He'd disappeared, in winter, too, just like Ramona Orlitzki. And when he'd turned up, he was floating in the river.

He'd had lots of people who cared about him, Alberg remembered. Just like Ramona Orlitzki.

He gazed at the photograph of his daughters that hung on the wall next to him, and thought about the graduation presents he'd bought for them. Maybe he should have phoned Maura, asked her advice. After all, he thought gloomily, he didn't get to see his daughters all that often. What made him think he could choose extra-special presents for them without help?

A little later, Isabella tapped at his door and immediately opened it, looking harassed. "I've made four phone calls so far. Nobody's seen her yet. The librarian's here."

"Don't worry, Isabella. We'll find her. Show Cassandra in, will you? In a minute," he called out, as Isabella retreated into the hall. "Give me a minute, first."

He piled the papers that littered his desk into several neat stacks. Hung up his jacket. Hauled the venetian blinds right to the top of the window. He was fervently grateful, for once, for

Isabella; there was no dust in his office, no grungy circles on his desk, no cigarette butts in the ashtray on the coffee table.

He ran his hands over his blond hair, straightened up, and pulled in his stomach. Then, what the hell, he thought, and let it out again.

There was a knock, and the door opened. "Right in there," said Isabella, from the hall.

"Thank you," said Cassandra Mitchell, and stepped inside.

Alberg looked at her for a long time, smiling. She smiled back, and he thought she blushed.

"Well for heaven's sake," she said. "Hello."

"You look so damn good," said Alberg. He walked toward her, trying not to think about anything, and put his arms around her.

Cassandra closed her eyes and let her cheek rest against his chest. She could feel or hear his heart beating, and then he pressed her hard against him and she felt her own heartbeat, too, and she couldn't tell which was which. One was beating much faster than the other; that one's mine, she thought. She lifted her head, eyes still closed. Delicately her fingers touched the nape of his neck, and slowly she pulled his face toward hers. She had been waiting for this for months and months, a kiss from Karl Alberg with no Roger in the way, no Roger in her heart; Roger was gone, all right, she thought, tasting Alberg, losing herself in this, a sweet, clean kiss, with power in it. . . .

She pulled away but held on to his shoulders. She was glad he was big. A substantial man, she thought fondly. His face looked a little older than when they had first met, his hair was a little thinner, he was still enigmatic—until he smiled. She remembered the first time he'd kissed her—in her kitchen, in the dark, while outside the moon flirted with clouds and shone when it could upon the water. He'd been cockier then; more certain of himself. Or brash, and only pretending certainty. She touched his face with her fingertips and remembered being afraid to go to bed with him then because she thought she would tell him anything, there; but was there anything, now, that she wouldn't want him to know?

"Let's go have some lunch," she said, smiling up at him.

Alberg linked his arms around her waist. "Let's go to Victoria."

"Victoria?" said Cassandra, laughing. "For lunch?"

"Not today. Friday. For the weekend."

Cassandra shook her head. "That's moving a little fast, don't you think?"

"Fast, hell." Gently, he pulled her closer. "You like flowers, right? I happen to know that in Victoria there are all kinds of flowers blooming."

"Pansies," said Cassandra. She leaned against him.

"Oh, yeah?"

"Primroses. Bergenia. Broom."

He pushed her away, so as to look at her. "There, see?" said Alberg, beaming.

"How did you know?"

"Sid Sokolowski was over there the other day. He takes an interest in plants and things."

"But there's no need to go all the way to Victoria," said Cassandra. She put her arms around him. "The periwinkle in my rock garden is already out."

"And if the sun shines," Alberg went on, his cheek resting on the top of her head, "the ocean in Victoria will be extremely blue."

"I don't know," said Cassandra.

She heard Alberg sigh.

Cassandra smiled, holding him close.

"I'd pay," he said hopefully.

"Oh, well then," said Cassandra. "Why didn't you say so?"

C H A P T E R

12

"Death. And diaries. And money," Benjamin repeated. "That's what we've got to talk about."

A winter rain was falling on the Sunshine Coast, and the breeze from the ocean was cold and damp. Leaves from the arbutus trees blew across the patio, making scouring sounds, like a coarse broom scraping a concrete floor. Every so often the wind sent a spray of sea water over the barrier made of rock, right onto the patio, and some of the spray struck the window with a sizzling sound, as though the ocean water were hot instead of cold.

Benjamin was sitting in Zoe's black leather chair, waiting for her to say something. His head rested against the backrest, his ugly hands rested on the arms, and his eyes were closed. But Zoe knew that his body was rigid with the strain of apprehension. She heard in his breathing a struggle not to gasp.

She had known instantly what he was talking about. And she had instantly believed him; Benjamin, preposterous as it seemed, was in possession of something that could just possibly harm her.

She gazed at him dispassionately, thinking.

She thought she might decide to sit there, quietly, silently, for a long time, until he was compelled to burst from the chair, crouched and cornered, panting like an animal.

She had underestimated him, she thought, noting that perspiration had appeared on his forehead, gleaming.

More information was required.

"Imagine that," she said aloud. "You've had them all this time," said Zoe, "and you never said a word."

"I was saving it." Benjamin cleared his throat.

"I guess it's your last card." She studied him thoughtfully. "You must need money very badly."

"All I want from you is the Great North stock," said Benjamin doggedly. "Which is rightfully mine anyway."

Zoe shook her head. "Not anymore it isn't. I paid you for it. More than it was worth, as a matter of fact."

"But I was right, wasn't I," said Benjamin quickly. "It's tripled in value. Just like I told you it would. You owe me something for that, surely."

"No." Zoe looked away from him, out the window. She couldn't see the horizon. Too much rain was falling into the ocean. Everything was gray and blurry. "No," she said. "I don't owe you anything at all."

"I'd only sell half," said Benjamin. He was begging, Zoe noticed with interest. That was pleasant. "I'd keep the other half," he said. "It would stay in the family, if that's what you're worried about."

Zoe laughed. "I want it to stay with me, Benjamin. Th
what I want."

"I get the shares," he said, "and you get your diaries. It':
fair exchange."

"They aren't diaries," said Zoe. "They're scribblers. Book
I scribbled in from time to time. That's all they are."

Benjamin leaned toward her. "But you know what's ir
them. In one of them."

She didn't answer.

"It's all down there," he said in a low voice.

"Don't be melodramatic," said Zoe.

"Every detail," said Benjamin, in a whisper.

He sounded almost excited, thought Zoe. Probably because
he had the notion he was about to be rich again.

"I am certainly annoyed that you have my scribblers," she
said. "But I am not nearly annoyed enough to hand over to you
half a million dollars' worth of stock. I'm amazed that you
thought I'd even consider doing such a thing." She stood up,
exasperated, tired of sitting still. Hands on her hips, she stared
out the window. "What do you think you can do to me? It's
such a waste of time, listening to your twaddle."

"I can take your diary to the police. It's the RCMP, in
Sechelt, isn't it? I'll take it to the Mounties."

Zoe whirled on him, and he flinched. She became still then,
trying to control herself. "It is not a diary." She was still angry;
she could hear it in her voice. She longed to change her clothes
and go for a run in the rain. She took a deep breath and
squeezed her left hand with her right, five times. "They
wouldn't do anything with it," she went on, more calmly.
"They would simply think you were mad, trying to peddle such
a thing."

"Not peddling it," he said. "I'd be giving it to them."

"They'd be awfully curious to know why you'd decided to take this action now," said Zoe, "after hanging on to the silly thing for so many years." She squeezed her right hand with her left, five times.

"I'll tell them I just found it," he said. "In a trunk in the basement. While clearing away some old stuff."

"They'd think you were disgusting to want to humiliate your own sister." Zoe turned her back on him and looked out the window. "I was a mere child when it happened, for God's sake."

"Zoe. You wouldn't just be humiliated. You'd be prosecuted. They'd send you to jail."

"Oh, prosecuted—are you mad?" The wind was blowing harder now. Arbutus leaves clattered across the patio in a frenzy, chased by rain and seaspray. "I was a child," said Zoe. She wanted to laugh, but she didn't. "Prosecuted. Don't be ridiculous."

Benjamin got out of the chair and stood next to her. "Zoe. They'll check what you wrote in your diary—"

Zoe turned around. "I told you," she said coldly. "It is not a diary. I have never in my life kept a diary. Keeping a diary is a weak and feeble enterprise."

Benjamin stepped back. But he went on talking. "Believe me, Zoe. It's very serious," he said, stammering a little, as Zoe continued to stare at him. "You know it is. If I go to the police..." He took another step backward. "They'll investigate, all right. They will."

I could move, thought Zoe, staring at him. Just pick up and move.

But she had thoroughly enjoyed living here, these seven

years. She had had every intention of remaining here for the rest of her life.

Things simply cannot go on like this, she thought, with this idiot brother crawling out of the woodwork every time he goes broke or loses a spouse.

"I need some time," she said. "I have to think about it."

"There's really nothing to think about, though, Zoe, is there?" he said.

He was hanging on to the back of that damn chair, she noticed, for dear life. Did he think she was going to go berserk and attack him with her fingernails, for heaven's sake?

"Benjamin," she said firmly, "you've had my scribblers for—what, twenty years? More. You've had more than twenty years to read them, pore over them, think about what's in them. Figure out how to use them."

She walked out of the living room and waited for him in the foyer.

"I need some time," she said, "to get used to this." She opened the front door. "Get out of here. Come back in two days. And not a moment sooner."

CHAPTER

13

Late the following morning Cassandra Mitchell heard a loud knocking on her front door. She was immediately awake. As she hurried to the door, tying her robe, she told herself that it couldn't be somebody from the hospital; they would phone if they needed to get in touch with her. But well-meaning people sometimes insisted on delivering bad news face to face, instead of impersonally over a telephone line, and when she pulled open the door she was praying that it wouldn't be Alex Gillingham standing there.

"Thank God," she said, when it turned out to be Karl Alberg.

"I heard about your mother. How bad is it?"

"I don't know," she said wearily. "I never know."

"May I come in?"

She stood back, and when he'd stepped across the threshold she closed the door and leaned against it.

"I woke you up. I'm sorry."

"It's all right." Cassandra combed her hair back from her forehead with her fingers. She couldn't remember if she'd taken off her mascara before going to bed. Oh God there's probably mascara all over my face, she thought, and then she remembered that of course she hadn't put any on, not to rush off to the hospital in the dead of night.

"How about if I make you some coffee," said Alberg, taking off his jacket.

"I'd like that," said Cassandra, feeling slightly cheered.

Alberg took her by the elbow and led her into the living room.

"That smells nice," she said, sniffing the air. "What is it?"

"Oh, it's something one of my kids gave me. Aftershave lotion or something. I don't know what the hell it is. You're probably allergic to it." He sat her down on the white leather sofa.

"I'm not allergic to a single solitary thing," said Cassandra. "Not that I know of, anyway."

"Hey, did I tell you they're graduating? Next week. In Calgary. Mortarboards and everything. Shit, I can't believe it," he said, smiling broadly. He glanced toward the end of the room, where sliding glass doors led to the patio. "Are those locked? I noticed your front door wasn't," he said disapprovingly.

"Oh God, Karl," she said. She wanted to laugh but felt too tired.

"Okay, okay. I hope you've got one of those drip things," he said, going to the kitchen. "That's the only kind of coffeepot I know how to use."

"Didn't Mountie school teach you anything, for heaven's

sake? I thought for sure you'd have learned how to ride a horse. Skin a caribou. Trap a beaver. And make boiled coffee. Even I know how to make boiled coffee."

He looked at her reproachfully through the doorway to the kitchen. "Of course I learned how to ride a horse. I got my training in the old days." He disappeared again, and Cassandra heard him opening cupboards.

"It's the one to the left of the sink," she told him.

Her feet were getting cold, so she got up from the sofa to fetch slippers from her bedroom. While she was in there she opened the curtains. She brushed her hair in front of the mirror, tied her robe more tightly around her, and turned to leave the room. Then she looked down at the unmade bed. Sheets, blankets, pillows, and bedspread sprawled there invitingly, warm and wanton. It was a queen-sized bed, which was good, she thought, because he was a big man. She flushed, staring at the bed.

"Have you got a tray somewhere?" he called out.

Quickly she left the bedroom, closing the door behind her. "Yes," she said. "I'll get it."

A few minutes later they sat side by side on the sofa, drinking coffee. "Have you found Ramona yet?" said Cassandra.

Alberg shook his head.

"Karl," she said, turning to him. "My God. I was sure she'd have turned up by now. It's been a day and a night."

"We've checked with everybody we can think of. Everybody Gillingham can think of. Everybody Isabella can think of. There's not a sign of her."

"Well, but . . . What do you think?"

Alberg shrugged. "She could have wandered off into the bush, I guess. Or maybe she found a place to hole up. It depends on how alert she is."

"She kind of drifts in and out, I think."

"Yeah."

"She's not in her house? I heard the tenants—"

"Yeah. Hawaii. No, we got a key and checked the place out, Sid Sokolowski did; nobody inside. So Christ knows where she is."

"What do you do now?"

He put down his coffee cup and stretched his arm along the back of the sofa. "We do a full-scale search. And we've got a description out up and down the Coast. Eventually somebody will spot her. It's all we can do."

She reached over to squeeze his hand. "This is good coffee."

"Naturally it's good coffee."

"Do you cook anything?"

"Of course I cook. How do you think I eat?"

"In restaurants."

"Of course I cook. I've got some specialties that would make you drool."

"Name one."

"Meat loaf."

"Meat loaf. Hmm. Do you want an ashtray?"

He gave her an injured look. "Don't you remember? I quit. Before you went away."

"I remember. But I thought you might have started again."

"Not this fella. Six months, it's been."

"Good for you, Karl."

"Now," he said softly. "Tell me about your mother."

Cassandra put down her cup. "She called me at two in the morning. She thought she was having a heart attack. I phoned for an ambulance, and it got to her house before I did. I followed them to the hospital and waited for a couple of hours. When they finally let me in to see her she was asleep."

"Was it a heart attack?"

"Alex Gillingham says no." She glanced up at Alberg. "It's happened before, Karl. But he says there's nothing actually wrong with her."

"But every time it happens, you think this time it'll be different, it'll be serious."

"Right," said Cassandra. "Exactly. I go through the same crap, every time. I'm out of my mind with worry and at the same time I'm angry with her. I phone my brother in Edmonton and he says 'Should I come out?' and I really want to say 'Yes, yes, for God's sake,' but I don't, I say, 'Let's wait and see,' and the next day or the day after that she's fine again and I call him and say 'Stay home.' " There were tears in her eyes; she flicked them from her face." I do love her, but she drives me crazy. I'm always gritting my teeth when I'm with her, and then something like this happens. . . ."

Alberg pulled her close to him. "It's all right," he said, and rocked her in his arms.

She felt comforted, and eventually she became drowsy. She thought she might fall asleep right there, cuddled against his chest.

But then a change occurred. There was an imperceptible alteration in the situation. And Cassandra was wide awake again, all five senses on the alert. She thought about her unmade bed. Maybe it still smelled of the honeysuckle bath powder she'd used before going to bed last night.

His hand moved inside her robe; his face was extremely near; his lips opened before he kissed her; and then the telephone rang.

"Shit," said Alberg, and then, "Sorry," because after all it could have been the hospital.

But it was Isabella.

"I just got back here from lunch," she said. "There's still no news about Ramona. And then I find out you're late."

"Late? What the hell am I late for?"

"For Bernie Peters. Do you want to find yourself a cleaning lady or don't you? She's here right now. Waiting. Been waiting for twenty minutes, she tells me. And she's got somebody to do for at eleven-thirty. Did anybody check with the liquor store?"

Alberg closed his eyes and tried to concentrate. "About what, Isabella?"

"About Ramona. She'd want to get herself some gin. I told you about Ramona and her gin."

Alberg's eyes opened. "That's a very good idea, Isabella. I'll check it out."

"But first you'll be getting yourself back here toot sweet, won't you."

"I confess that I forgot about Bernie Peters, Isabella," he said bleakly. "Do I really have to see her now?"

"She's a woman much in demand," said Isabella.

"Fuck it," said Alberg.

"I beg your pardon, Staff Sergeant?" said Isabella. "I can t believe that I heard you say that."

"I'm coming," he said grimly, and hung up.

Cassandra handed him his jacket. She touched the slight cleft in his chin. "Thank you, Karl," she said.

When he got back to the detachment, Bernie Peters had left.

"And I won't guarantee," said Isabella, with massive disapproval, "that I'll ever be able to get her back here, either."

CHAPTER

14

Zoe Strachan had never been interested in music. Then one day she was walking along Robson Street in Vancouver and she heard something that reached out and seized her.

It was being played by a man with a strange, many-stringed instrument. Zoe stopped, and listened. When it was over she asked the musician what he had played, and when she returned to Sechelt later that day she had bought a tape featuring Pachelbel's "Canon."

When she got home she played it over and over again, listening with intense concentration.

As she listened Zoe saw bars, close together like a fence. They reached higher than she could see, and lower than she could see. They were slim and silver and gleaming, and she knew that they were indestructible. And as she listened Zoe also saw, behind the bars, feathery flashes of fire that swept between them and entwined themselves around them. The fire, she saw, had freedom enough to flutter and sweep, but was imprisoned behind the bars. Yet as she continued to listen the bars became flame, and the plumes of fire became bars.

She decided that the music was talking about a struggle resolved.

So on the day that Benjamin announced his intention to blackmail her, Zoe had again put on Pachelbel's "Canon," and listened, and listened.

It was fully dark outside when she turned off the tape player. For a while she sat in her living room without turning on the lights; deliberating.

Most people made up their lives as they went along, but Zoe didn't have that luxury. It was the only thing she envied about other people, the permission they held to improvise their days without fear of disaster. It was a gift of which they were apparently unaware. The gift of extemporaneous life.

Zoe couldn't afford to extemporize. She was extrinsic to the world in which she found herself, and there was great peril in this.

Like the fire in the "Canon," Zoe thought, I have erected bars to live behind, because they give to my life structure, and security.

She was pleased with this image.

She pulled the curtains, switched on the lights, and went into the kitchen.

She would have something to eat, she thought, and watch the six o'clock news, while she tried to figure out how to kill her brother.

CHAPTER

15

Ramona was lucky; he hadn't even come into the house that first time. There she sat, her heart choked right up into her throat, holding that mug of instant coffee, and she waited, and she waited, but nothing happened. It was a long time before she heard the car door open and close and the engine start and the car drive off again. She couldn't figure out what this person, whoever he was, had been up to all that time. Probably peering in the windows.

When he left she scurried out and got her shopping bag.

She still hadn't felt safe, though. So she got some cheese and crackers and went back into the closet.

Later in the day another car stopped on the gravel, or maybe it was the same one. This time the fellow came right inside, a big tall man by the sounds of him; he clunked through the house, and every so often he called out, "Anybody here? Mrs. Orlitzki? Are you here?" He identified himself, said he was from the RCMP. You could tell he felt foolish, talking to an empty house.

He hadn't even opened the closet door, as it turned out.

That time when he went away Ramona did feel safe. She crept around the house, closing the curtains. Then she dragged her old rocking chair out of the bedroom where Marcia and Robbie had moved it and put it back in the living room, where it belonged.

Ramona spent the rest of the day recovering from her exertions, which had been considerable. She dozed off for a while, in the rocking chair. When she woke up she made herself some tea and ate some more cheese and crackers and dozed off again. For dinner she opened a can of ravioli, which was pretty awful but filling.

She kept peeking out the bedroom window at the house next door, but the Ferrises stayed in all day, and all evening too.

When she awakened on Thursday morning, at first she didn't know where she was, but that soon passed, and then she felt belligerent and triumphant, and marveled at herself.

After she'd had her wake-up coffee, she used the bathroom. She sat on the toilet for a long time, daydreaming. It was a luxury she was thoroughly appreciating, to be able to sit there until your bottom went numb if you liked, without some nurse coming knocking on the door to make sure you hadn't fallen in and drowned. Eventually, though, she felt a craving for some TV soap opera. She stirred, fumbled for the toilet paper, and pulled off the last few inches of the roll. Awkwardly, she reached around and opened the cupboard under the sink. There was half a box of Kleenex there, thank goodness, but no toilet paper. Ramona used the Kleenex.

Once out of the bathroom, she searched the house. There wasn't another roll of toilet paper in the place. And no more Kleenex, either.

Well that settled it. She could do without fruit, she could even do without gin, at least for a while. But she certainly couldn't do without t.p.

And luck was with her. Not more than half an hour later, she was sitting in front of the TV, watching "The Young and the Restless," devoutly grateful that Marcia's mother, Reba McLean, paid for the kids to have cable, when she heard some activity going on next door.

She hustled into the bedroom and peered cautiously out between the curtain and the edge of the window. Sure enough, the Ferrises were getting set to go off somewhere. Harold helped his wife into their car, and placed the white dog on her lap, and made his way around to the driver's door. Then the car pulled out onto the highway and lurched off toward Sechelt, and Ramona was out of her house like a shot.

There wasn't anybody on the beach.

The couple who lived on the other side of her both worked; she'd heard them leaving their house early in the morning.

Ramona sneaked over to the Ferrises' back door and found it unlocked.

She took only what she needed, promising herself that she'd make things right with them later. She took one apple, one orange, and one banana. She took a can of apple juice. She took a four-roll package of toilet paper and a large box of Kleenex.

And she took a bottle of gin.

She loaded her booty into a brown paper bag and lugged it back to her house.

In the afternoon, sitting in her chair, looking out the

window at the sea, Ramona began wondering exactly *how* she was going to make things right with the Ferrises. She'd stolen from them, after all. She was horrified. However could she make it up to them? She began to feel panicky, just thinking about it . . . then she couldn't remember what day it was . . . Thursday, she thought finally, relieved, and then—oh my goodness I have to get moving. . . .

Ramona got a little stiffly to her feet and looked around, bewildered. She spotted a heavy coat; but surely she wouldn't need that. She carried it outside with her, though, and it was a good thing she did, too, it was nippy out there—nippy, nothing; it was positively cold. Aghast, Ramona looked up at the bleak sky—a winter sky. How had it gotten to be winter? She was on her way to meet Rosie, but it was winter. . . . She stopped and pressed the palm of her hand against her forehead and squeezed her eyes tight shut for a few seconds. Then she continued making her way along the beach, the sand sucking at her shoes, past three houses—she knew them, recognized them . . . but where was Rosie? She reached the place where the shore curved inward to form a shallow bay and the bush came right down to the sand; this piece of land was owned by the government—or was it the Indians? She couldn't remember. She couldn't remember very much of anything. There was a lot of clamoring going on in her brain. She tried to be calm and let her brain work things out on its own, but she was very very tired.

Ramona tottered up the slight rise from the beach and slumped against the trunk of a colossal Douglas fir. She leaned there, panting, for a minute. Then she sat down on the ground, on a carpet of needles, her back against the treetrunk. The tree felt very . . . authentic, very substantial; she could almost feel its ancient heart beating, slow and steady. She was aware of the fragrance of the fir trees, and the sound of the ocean lapping at the sand below her, and the rain-moisture in the air. . . . Then there was a swooshing inside her, and with a certainty that was dizzying, almost nauseating, she knew her world once more.

She wept for a while. From relief, or from fear; she wasn't sure which. But then she told herself that she had to be staunch. No matter what.

She saw that she was on the Strachan woman's property, at the beginning of the promontory, not far from the highway.

Ramona wasn't about to walk along that beach again. She'd return to her house via the road and take her chances on being spotted.

A few minutes later she clambered to her feet and aimed herself down the Strachan woman's driveway toward the highway, where she stopped again, to rest for a moment against another tree.

She'd be grateful to be back in her own house, that was for sure.

Even though it wasn't really her own house at the moment, not with other people's belongings scattered here and there.

Just as Ramona pushed herself away from the tree, a person shot out of the driveway at a gallop. Ramona shrank back, both hands clutching at her chest. But it turned out not to be a gallop, exactly, more like a lope, and it was the Strachan woman herself doing it. Ramona didn't think she'd even seen her. Dressed in blue denim and sneakers she ran, jogged, out of her driveway and made a sharp left, and off she went up the highway, her black hair bouncing on her shoulders, and before Ramona even came to her senses about it she was staring at the woman's retreating back.

Enough's enough for one damn day, she thought firmly, and

set off in a crablike scurry, because her thighs ached and her knees hurt, down the road toward her house.

When she got there she was breathless and sore, and chilly despite the vigorous exercise she'd undergone. She decided to make herself some instant coffee.

While she was waiting for the kettle to boil she noticed the spider plant hanging by the kitchen window.

There were a couple of ferns in the bedroom, too, she remembered.

And a cluster of African violets on a table in the living room.

She started to wonder where the policeman had gotten the key to let himself in.

Ramona sank into a chair at the kitchen table. Her knees were trembling, and there was a great echo inside her head.

Her house wasn't a haven at all.

She was going to have to find another place to hide.

CHAPTER

16

Zoe ran almost every day.

This Thursday afternoon, as she ran along the shoulder of the highway, she wondered for a moment about the stress of running, wondered how her joints were holding up. Sometimes her right knee gave her trouble.

There was moisture in the air, although it wasn't exactly raining, and it felt cool and refreshing against her face. She took off her earmuffs and gloves and stuffed them into the big pocket in the front of her sweatshirt.

It was unlikely that she'd be able to find out where Benjamin had hidden her scribblers. Even if she got him thoroughly drunk, he'd probably manage to lie.

It was good to be thinking about this while running, she thought. The frustration it produced got turned into physical energy that was immediately consumed.

He was so stupid to have believed that she would let him get away with this.

She had reached the place where the highway took a curve to accommodate an enormous Sitka spruce; this was the one-mile mark. She approached the tree and pressed the palm of her right hand against its trunk, then pressed the palm of her left hand there. Then she turned and headed back toward her house.

She had planned and worked too hard for peace, seclusion—a life that was precisely the life she wanted. All put at risk, now, by this ineffectual, nonproductive man who wasn't worth the powder it would cost to blow him up.

She couldn't see blowing him up. She didn't know enough about explosives. And although she could learn, death by explosion was certain to alarm the authorities.

She could poison him, she thought, and considered this for a while, as she ran.

But she didn't know anything about poisons, either, and unless she could manage to get hold of some that was absolutely undetectable, she oughtn't to consider it. Death by poison, too, would cause a lot of consternation.

At least he didn't have a wife or a family to ask questions afterward.

She swiped at her forehead with her sleeve. Too bad he doesn't jog, she thought, panting. She could have challenged him to a race and tried to induce a heart attack.

It will have to be an accident, she decided, turning off the highway. She slowed to a trot, then a walk, for the last quarter mile across the promontory to her house.

If not a car accident, then something else.

It would come to her.

When she had showered and changed, she stood by the living room window, looking out at the rain. Killing Benjamin, it occurred to her, might be considerably more complicated and difficult than the only alternative, which was to kill herself.

What if she killed him but got caught, and ended up going to jail for the rest of her life? Dying would be far preferable to that.

She wasn't fond of pain. But she knew she could find a way to do it without causing herself physical suffering.

She would have to decide how to dispose of her money, though. She certainly wouldn't want Benjamin, or the government, getting any of it. Perhaps she ought to convert everything she had to cash, transfer it to her checking account, and divide it among the listings in the Sechelt phone book.

She roamed uneasily through her house, stroking her favorite pieces of furniture, turning television sets on and off. There were all these possessions, too. What would become of them? How on earth could she dispose of all her belongings— her car, her house, for heaven's sake? Could she get rid of all these things without calling attention to herself?

Her house. Her fortress.

She had chosen the Sunshine Coast as her home because it was made remote from metropolitan Vancouver by the need to get there by ferry.

She chose Sechelt because it was in the middle of the Coast, halfway between the ferry at Langdale, which crossed Howe Sound to Horseshoe Bay, and the one at Powell River, which crossed Georgia Strait to Vancouver Island.

She had looked for a long time, and then bought the waterfront property, and then she bought the lots on either side of it, and the lots on either side of them, too; she bought the whole promontory. It wasn't a huge area—less than two acres. Manageable in size. The highway formed its eastern border, so she never had to worry about acquiring neighbors.

She'd had a plain house built, with exactly the amount of room in it that she needed. And a garage.

And halfway up the driveway, a small guest cottage. It wasn't used often. Just once or twice a year.

One of the things she'd had to check out before deciding to move here was whether there were enough bars. She found four up and down the Coast that would do, not counting whatever there might be in Sechelt; that would have been too close to home.

Sex, to Zoe, was a hunger, the satisfaction of which depended not on appetite but on need. She felt it first when she was fourteen and a boy three years ahead of her in school began following her home. One day he caught up with her and took her into a park. What followed was not a particularly pleasant experience for Zoe, but it proved in the end an adequate introduction to the gratification of sexual desire.

Every few months she dressed up in one of her costumes and went to a bar. She found someone, took him to her guest cottage, and they had sex. Zoe did it thoroughly, and with energy, the way she did everything. Afterward, she sent the person on his way.

She told these men that her elderly parents lived in the house by the water.

Everything had worked out extremely well. Each aspect of her life was precisely as she had planned it.

She was damned if she was going to let Benjamin destroy it.

Late that afternoon, the skies cleared. Zoe sat in her office, in an enormous round chair made of bamboo, which had a huge, sumptuous rust-colored cushion. She sat cross-legged, holding a glass of chardonnay. The sun was in the process of setting, preparing to sizzle itself out in the waters of the ocean. Zoe watched it burning in her wine.

It was time to insist upon some single-minded exertion from her brain.

Zoe had complete confidence in her brain, and treated it with respect. She tried to understand it and anticipate its needs. She kept her body healthy so as to spare her brain the distraction of worrying about disease or injury to its host. She kept herself as tranquil as possible, thereby providing a close to ideal environment in which her brain could work. It was like maintaining a greenhouse for an exotic plant, or a climate-controlled garage in which to house a fine automobile.

The sun set; the wineglass warmed in her hand. She closed her eyes and rocked gently back and forth and thought about accidents. Car accidents, boating accidents, industrial accidents, skiing accidents; accidents with farm equipment, accidents with chain saws, accidents with sharp knives, or long-bladed scissors, or drugs; accidents that crushed, or pierced, or punctured, or impaled. She imagined him bleeding, suffocating, choking. She imagined him crumpling to the floor, collapsing into coma, fluttering into death. She saw him crumple . . . collapse. . . . She saw him fall.

She thought she knew just how it would feel to place the palms of her hands against his shoulderblades and push, strongly. She thought she knew just what he would look like, plummeting through the air, his scream a wisp, a thin stream of white breath that might even continue to hang in the air for a second or two after his body had struck the rocks, and she would bend over, carefully, to see if any part of him was still moving, down there on the rocks where he had crashed. . . .

Zoe opened her eyes and smiled.

She would push him off the cliff right outside his own front door.

They would meet at the house in West Vancouver. He would give her the scribblers, and she would turn over the stock certificates, ensuring that he put them somewhere other than in his pocket. They would have a drink, and she would make certain that he got thoroughly drunk, if he wasn't drunk already, which he probably would be. After a while she would get up to leave. When she got to her car she would pretend that it wouldn't start. She would ask Benjamin to look at it, and when he got out of the elevator in the parking area at the top of the cliff, she would push him over, retrieve the certificates, and head for Horseshoe Bay and the ferry.

Zoe got out of the big round chair and went to the window. There was still a faint glow in the sky. The days, she thought, must be getting longer. Soon it would be spring again.

CHAPTER
17

Her brother was already on the scene when she arrived, his place in the household comfortably staked out.

They named her with the very last letter in the alphabet. He'd probably had something to do with that.

None of the ordinary names had seemed right, they told her. So they'd had to go right to the end of the alphabet. The last name in the world, that was the name they'd given her: Zoe.

Benjamin was four years older, and sometimes he made her so mad she hit him. Usually he'd just shrug his shoulders and go away then, but sometimes she hit him so hard that it hurt him, and he started to hit her back. Once he made her nose bleed. So she leaned over the sofa and shook her head hard so that the blood would go all over the sofa and he'd get into real trouble, which he did.

Zoe didn't like him, and she didn't dislike him.

She had private places indoors that he didn't know about, and she wanted one outdoors, as well. A place from which she could survey the world without being seen, by Benjamin or anybody else.

In her yard there was a pool to swim in, a gazebo to sit in, but nowhere to play. There were rose gardens and vegetable gardens and rhododendron plantings beneath the trees and a little brook that cut across the property at its lower end—spring bulbs bloomed here in great profusion. But there wasn't a tree fit for climbing or a secret place fit for hiding herself in.

So when she was eight, just after she'd gotten her first scribbler, she went poking around on the neighbors' property, which was just as big as hers but a lot less tended. It rolled up and then down again at the very back, and on that little hill were several fruit trees. Zoe climbed the back fence and sneaked up through the brush to the top of the hill, where the orchard began. From there she could see the whole back part of the property, and over the fence at the side into her own yard, as well.

This became her secret place. She would climb a tree and wedge herself in between a thick branch and the trunk, and if it was the right season she'd stuff herself with cherries or apples while she sat there, feeling like a big strong bird in its nest.

Four years passed, and Zoe grew and grew, but she didn't grow too big to nestle in the branches of a tree, and she didn't grow too old to need a secret place.

Two old people lived in the big old house at the front of the property. They never bothered picking the cherries or the apples, but sometimes their grown-up children came for a visit, and they'd take some of the fruit away with them.

One day when she was twelve, Zoe was sitting in an apple tree. It was July, and the apples were pretty well ready to eat; they were larger than a tennis ball, not as big as a softball, still green but starting to look yellowish.

Zoe was digging her fingernail into the treetrunk and scooping away little pieces of it, which she then flicked toward the ground. She'd been doing this for quite a while. She had dug through all of the tree's layers of skin and was now picking away at what she figured must be muscle.

From time to time she wrapped her arms around the tree and rubbed her cheek hard against its trunk. Her cheek had begun to sting, and when she put her fingers on it they came away with a small amount of blood on them, as well as dirt, so the next time she hugged the tree she did it with the other side of her face against the trunk.

It had always been very important to Zoe that things be even. Sometimes at the dinner table she might catch herself tapping her right toe against the floor, for instance, and then she had to try to figure out how many times she'd done it without noticing, so that she could tap her left toe the same number of times.

After a while from her perch in the apple tree she noticed that the old woman, whose name was Mrs. Nelson, had come out of the house and was standing on her back porch, holding a straw hat in her hand. She put the hat on and tied its brown ribbons under her chin—and then she looked up the hill into the orchard.

Zoe became motionless.

Mrs. Nelson went slowly down the steps, holding on to the railing, and walked through the wildness of her flower garden, which didn't have any neat edges, toward the fruit trees. She stopped every so often to look at one of the flowers, but she always started to walk again, straight toward the apple tree where Zoe crouched.

The old people never picked the fruit from these trees, never; what did she think she was going to do, anyway, that old woman: get herself a ladder and climb up here to get herself some apples, or what? Zoe tried to move behind the treetrunk but couldn't find a branch in the right place to sit on. The leaves of the apple tree rustled when she moved, and she was afraid that Mrs. Nelson had heard them, even though she was still pretty far away.

Mrs. Nelson was wearing a brown-and-white dress, and she had white sandals on her feet. She stopped at the bottom of the little hill and sat on a wooden bench that faced the house. After a while she reached down and over and picked up an apple that had fallen from a tree and rolled there. She rubbed it on the skirt of her dress and took a bite of it and sat there for several more minutes, eating the apple. Then she put the core on the ground and stood up.

When she got too close, Zoe threw an apple at her.

Even though it didn't hit her, it made the old woman glance up into the trees. So Zoe threw another apple. This one struck Mrs. Nelson on the arm and surprised her a lot; Zoe watched it happen on her face when she had the idea that maybe the apples weren't falling on their own, maybe somebody was actually throwing them.

Zoe could see that this was hard for Mrs. Nelson to believe, so she threw another one, which hit the old woman on the shoulder. It must have landed harder than the first one because Mrs. Nelson said "Uh," and bent over, one hand fumbling out to the side until it came in contact with a treetrunk. She hobbled over and leaned against it, holding on to her shoulder.

"Who's there?" she said in a quivery voice. "Is there somebody up there?"

Zoe wanted to shout, "No there's nobody up there it's God throwing apples at you!" But instead of shouting she threw another apple. This one struck the brim of Mrs. Nelson's hat, making it go all crooked on her head.

Then Zoe got very angry with herself. Why had she done this? Now Mrs. Nelson was squinting hard up into the trees, her little eyes poking into all the branches, sniffing and poking into every single apple tree, and—there! They hit Zoe right in the face, those beady little old-woman eyes.

"Zoe," said Mrs. Nelson, sounding amazed.

"Zoe Zoe Zoe!" yelled Zoe.

She climbed fast down from the tree and ran to the top of the hill and down the other side and over the fence into the Bradleys' yard, where Henry Bradley was mowing his father's lawn. She ran clear across the Bradleys' property, screaming, "Damn you Henry damn you Henry!" until she reached the road, and then she ran along the road until it curved and went in front of her own house. She ran inside and up the stairs to her room, where she opened her windows wide and threw herself onto her bed and, hot with humiliation and rage, thought about putting a curse or something on old Mrs. Nelson.

That night there was another Zoe meeting. They always had them right before dinner.

"Mrs. Nelson said you were throwing apples at her today," said Zoe's mother, sounding tired and sad.

Zoe shrugged. "I was up in a tree. Maybe some apples fell off it."

"You mean it was an accident?" said Zoe's father.

Zoe shrugged again. "They could've hit her. I don't know."

"She says you yelled at her," said her mother.

"I don't remember. I might have. She scared me."

"How did she scare you?" said her father.

"By sneaking up on me."

"I can't imagine Mrs. Nelson sneaking up on you, Zoe," said her mother.

Zoe didn't say anything.

"What happened to your face? It's all scraped."

"I rubbed it against a tree."

"Zoe, for God's sake . . ."

"What were you doing in her orchard anyway?" said her father.

"Playing." Her stomach was growling. "I'm hungry. Can't we eat now?"

Her mother gave a big sigh.

Zoe looked at the floor. She was standing on a rug that was mostly dark red, with lots of big flowers all over it. The rug was lying on top of a beige-colored carpet, which covered almost the entire house. "Can we have dinner now?" she said.

"Mrs. Nelson doesn't want you to go into her yard anymore," said Zoe's father.

I don't care what she wants, said Zoe inside herself. Outside, she let her head nod up and down.

Her father stroked her hair. "Okay," he said. "Go find Benjamin. Tell him it's dinnertime."

The next day she saw that the old people had had the tall grass in the orchard cut down. This was to make it easier for them to see Zoe. They knew she wouldn't stay out of their yard.

They must have spent all their time from then on watching out the windows. The second Zoe started to climb one of the apple trees, they came out onto the back porch and shouted at her to go away. And then they phoned up her parents.

But she kept on trying, even though her mother and her father got very upset about it.

They caught her every time, but it was interesting to see how far she could get before she heard their screen door bang open and one of them began hollering at her.

But soon it wasn't interesting anymore.

It made her more and more angry to be kept out of that yard.

Every day she got angrier about it, until one day she was so jammed full of anger it made her shake. She wanted to hit things, chop things, smash things. But there was nothing in her hands to do it with. So she ran and ran and ran, across her own backyard and around the house and over the front lawn to the road, and down the road until she couldn't run anymore and had to fall down on some stranger's grass, where she lay panting and panting, watched *by a big dog sitting under a tree, until finally her heart stopped beating so fast and she could feel the hot sun on the backs of her legs, and she pushed herself up and went home.*

She couldn't go tearing around like this all the time. She'd wreck her body. She had to think of something.

A curse, or something.

CHAPTER

18

"How do I know you've actually got them?" said Zoe to her brother on Friday afternoon. They were sitting in her living room.

"How else would I know what's in them?" said Benjamin.

"I'd like to have a look at them. Just to be certain."

He wagged a finger at her. "Don't be silly, Zoe."

"It is very much against my principles," she said crossly, "to buy anything, anything at all, sight unseen."

He shook his head. He watched her for a moment. "Well? How about it?" he said. "Do we have a deal?"

"Yes, Benjamin," said Zoe. "We have a deal."

He put on a very wide grin. She thought it might split his face in two.

"You won't regret it," he said. He massaged his hands, hideous hands, red and lumpy with eczema. Perhaps they caused him pain. She hoped so. "I'll bring them to you tomorrow," he said.

"No," said Zoe flatly.

Benjamin reached for his wineglass and saw that it was empty. "One more for the road," he said, picking it up by the stem, "and I'll be on my way."

"I don't want you here again," said Zoe. "I'll go to your house."

"I . . . actually, that's not very convenient," said Benjamin.

"Fine," said Zoe. She stood up. "Let's forget it, then."

"All right, all right." Benjamin waved his hand impatiently. "I'll work it out. What time?"

"In the evening," said Zoe. "The early evening."

"Okay," he said. "Now how about my drink?"

"You've finished the bottle," said Zoe.

"I'll go get another," said Benjamin, and he put down his glass. "Where do you keep it?"

"No," said Zoe. She stared down at him for a moment. "I'll do it," she said.

After all, she thought, he didn't have many more drinks left to drink.

She turned on the light at the top of the stairs and made her way down into the basement. The wine was kept in a small room on the left, and she headed for that door but then changed her mind and went for a moment into a large room, half of which was a workroom. A fifty-year-old sideboard with silverware drawers and candle slides awaited her here. Someone had painted it dark brown. Zoe could hardly wait to strip it down and see what its real skin looked like. She checked the shelves to make sure she had everything she needed—several grades of sandpaper, large tins of stripper, chisels, steel wool, the finishing sander, furniture oil . . .

"Hey," called Benjamin, from the top of the stairs.

She gritted her teeth at the sound of his voice.

"I'm coming," said Zoe. She turned off the light in the workroom and closed the door.

"What are you doing down there?"

As soon as he left she would open all the doors and windows, never mind the weather, to let clean air sweep the memory of Benjamin from her house.

"Getting the wine," she said.

She'd scour every surface he'd touched, scrub every floor he'd walked upon.

She went into the small, cool room where she kept the wine and selected a bottle of inexpensive California red.

"You're not up to anything, are you?" Benjamin was hanging on to the open door, peering down the stairs, his face slashed with shadow.

"Don't be ridiculous," said Zoe. She mounted the steps.

When she had almost reached the top, he stretched his arm across the doorway so that she couldn't pass. She looked up at him, astonished. He was grinning at her. Her heart began to pound.

"Will you kindly get out of my way?" she said, struggling for control.

"Say please," said Benjamin, smirking.

"You're being childish," said Zoe, and there was such anger in her that her voice shook.

"Pretty please," said Benjamin.

Zoe realized when she thought about it later that what happened next wasn't a defeat: she hadn't lost, she hadn't surrendered; she'd made a decision, that was all. She stared up into Benjamin's face and decided to stop struggling; to let anger take her. . . .

She hadn't had these feelings for years and years and years; she hadn't had them since childhood.

And Benjamin saw it, saw something, in her eyes. Benjamin would have done anything, given anything, to take back those two small words.

"Pretty please," he'd said, like a stupid child.

It happened very very fast.

Zoe's right foot was two steps from the top of the stairs, and her left foot was one step lower. She was holding the California red at the shoulder of the bottle. Elated, she swung the bottle back; savagely, she drove it cork-end first into his stomach.

"Oof," said Benjamin, as he let go of the doorjamb and clutched at himself. Zoe pulled back against the banister, to her right. Benjamin sank forward against Zoe's left thigh, and she could have saved him from falling just by keeping her leg braced.

Rage electrified her. She had forgotten how voluptuous it was, her anger. She lifted the bottle high and brought the bottom of it down on the back of his head, and at the same time pulled her left leg out from under him.

"Ahhh," said Benjamin, and he crashed clumsily, noisily, all the way down the stairs.

C H A P T E R

19

Zoe, hanging on to the doorjamb for support, lowered herself to the top step to wait for her heart to stop its banging. She stared down at Benjamin, lying on the concrete floor at the bottom of the stairs. It was a wonder he hadn't smashed against the banister and broken it to smithereens, she thought, grateful for small mercies.

He was very still.

After a while her heartbeat was almost normal, and the trembling in her arms and legs had subsided. She set the wine bottle on the floor in the hallway and made her way cautiously down into the basement.

She stepped over him and hunkered down, her slim skirt pulling up over her thighs. She noticed a gleam of blood trickling out from under his head. His head was attached to his neck at an angle that was manifestly odd.

She licked her dry lips. "Benjamin? Benjamin." She was almost certain that he was dead. But she gave his shoulder a poke. Here we have a completely useless individual, she thought, good for absolutely nothing at all, not even terribly bright. But he did have one thing going for him, and that was tenacity.

She poked him again. She took his wrist in her fingers, feeling for his pulse. She stood up and gave him a gentle kick in the ribs, watching as his body spasmed, listening for a moan of protest and not hearing one.

Yes, she thought, nodding. He's dead, all right. The man is dead.

The trickle of blood had formed a small pool.

"Well," said Zoe, looking at the blood, at his twisted neck. "That's that, then."

She wouldn't have enjoyed killing him so much, if she'd been merely carrying out her plan. Doing it on an impulse, feeling reckless and intemperate, had been enormously exciting. She had been sexually aroused. She hadn't expected that.

But she had a problem now. She had to consider carefully what to do.

Her sense of satisfaction began ebbing away.

It was almost three o'clock. Half an hour to the terminal— she could catch the three-thirty ferry if she got a move on. Half an hour from Horseshoe Bay to the house—maybe twenty minutes, if she was lucky. An hour to search the place. Then half an hour back to the terminal, catch the six-thirty ferry—she could be home by seven-thirty.

She went through his pockets, being careful not to move him around much or disturb the placid puddle of blood. She found his keys and took them. Then she hurried upstairs and grabbed a jacket from the hall closet.

She went outside, locked the front door, and rummaged

through his car, just in case he'd brought the scribblers with him, but of course he hadn't.

She felt herself rushing, and tried to slow down, tried to think clearly.

Four and a half hours he'd lie here, at the bottom of her basement stairs. And then what would she do with him?

Try to dump him in the sea?

Get the police, tell them there's been an accident? Of course she had to say it was an accident. What was the alternative?

But they'd want to know why she hadn't reported it earlier.

I'll think of something, she told herself, trying to unlock her car door. Eventually she realized she was attempting to open it with Benjamin's keys.

She fished her own keys out of her handbag with hands that she saw were shaking.

"Damn the man," she said, getting in the car. "Damn him to hell."

Okay, she told herself as she drove off her property and turned onto the highway.

Work it out.

He was drunk. You wouldn't let him drive in that condition. You told him to sleep it off, and you went out to buy some food for dinner.

She checked the time and pressed her foot down on the accelerator. If she missed the three-thirty ferry she might as well forget it; she couldn't leave him lying there for more than four and a half hours.

Where could she say she'd been, even for only four and a half hours? It wouldn't take more than an hour to buy food.

Think, Zoe, she told herself, flexing her hands on the steering wheel.

That damn stupid man, she thought, furious.

She was in Sechelt now. Thank God there wasn't much traffic. And she wouldn't have to worry about lineups at the ferry terminal, either, not on a weekday in January. The roads were dry, too; it was another gray day, but not a rainy one. And there was no fog, thank God.

She heard a siren and in the same moment saw flashing lights in her rearview mirror. Damn it to hell, thought Zoe, slowing and moving to the side of the road so it could pass her, whatever it was, an ambulance or a fire truck or something, but when she slowed down it did, too, and she saw that it was a police car. Incredulous, she brought her car to a stop and saw the police car pull in behind her.

She clutched at her forehead. "I cannot believe this," she said. "I refuse to believe this."

She looked into the rearview mirror and saw the policeman climb out of his car, taking his own sweet time about it, and she glanced at her watch, and she knew that she was not going to make it to Langdale in time.

And then Zoe felt her serenity emerge, resolute and glacial, from wherever it had temporarily hidden itself.

Okay, she thought.

This is it, then.

This is how it's going to be.

The police officer was tall and young, and as he walked toward her car Zoe saw that he enjoyed having broad shoulders and narrow hips and muscular thighs. She rolled down her window and watched his face as he met her eyes and recognized her. A few people in town recognized her. But not many of them had the nerve to look at her the way this police officer was looking at her. A frisson of something—sexual desire? *Lustmord?*—rippled along her spine. But it was too late to make any use of this, because it was too late to catch the ferry.

She waited, watching him. He took off his hat and ran his hand over his hair, which was black and curly. Zoe almost laughed, but she managed not to; she didn't even smile. She just pretended for the moment that she was in a bar, dressed up, camouflaged, hungry.

"Miss Strachan, isn't it?"

Zoe nodded.

"I'm afraid you were exceeding the speed limit back there."

"Oh, dear," said Zoe, gazing straight into his extremely blue eyes. He was cocksure, all right; she felt an urgent need to whittle him down a little. But instead she lifted her hands from the steering wheel and held them out toward him, diffidently, so that he could see the tremor in them. "I'm afraid I'm a little upset."

"I'm going to have to give you a ticket," he said with a smile, showing her his teeth, which didn't interest her in the slightest.

"My brother's had an accident," she said. She turned away to fumble in her handbag for a Kleenex. "I think—I'm afraid he's dead." She buried her nose in the tissue and permitted herself to weep.

"What kind of an accident? Where? Miss Strachan?"

Zoe felt his hand on her shoulder and sobbed harder. His dismay was almost palpable. Before he could pull himself together and become decisive, she turned her wet face to him and said, "He's fallen down my basement stairs. There's blood . . ." and began again to weep.

The policeman gave her shoulder a hasty squeeze. "I'll call for an ambulance," he said, and hurried back to his car.

Zoe sat stony and sullen, staring out the windshield.

After a while she heard him crunching across the gravel

shoulder toward her, and she sighed, and straightened, and dabbed delicately at her cheeks with the sodden Kleenex.

"They're going to meet us at your house," he said.

"Oh, good," whispered Zoe. "Thank you."

"Why didn't you phone somebody?" he said, leaning against her car.

"I don't have a telephone," said Zoe. "I hate telephones," she explained, giving him a smile. She started her car, and he drew back quickly. "You can give me the ticket when we get to my house." She put the engine in drive, signaled, and pulled out onto Sechelt's main street. In the mirror she saw the police officer trotting hastily back to his vehicle.

CHAPTER

20

"I've been thinking," said Alberg, pulling on his jacket. "You know what's good about the Ramona situation, Isabella?" He sat on the edge of her desk.

"She's been gone almost three days," Isabella said dismally.

"I know that. What's good about it is, we haven't got a body."

Isabella nodded. "That's true. We don't. Not yet anyway."

"I was afraid she might have gone off somewhere to do herself in."

Isabella nodded again. "I have to admit it, that occurred to me, too."

"But I don't think she's done that. Her body would have been found by now."

"Do you think so?"

"I do."

"Well, but—where do you think she is, then?"

"I haven't got a clue," said Alberg. "But I bet you a month's salary she's still alive, wherever she is. People wander away all the time, Isabella. You know that."

"The trouble with Ramona is," said Isabella, "that if she doesn't want to be found, you might not ever find her. Ramona's old; but she's smart. She forgets a thing or two; but she's smart."

Alberg shoved a new notebook into his inside pocket. "Yeah. But maybe we're smarter."

"Don't count on it," said Isabella.

"Maybe we'll get lucky, then. Or maybe she'll decide she wants to come back." He got up and started for the door. "Get hold of Gillingham, will you? Tell him to go out to the place at the end of Mills Road. Name's Strachan. Report of an accidental death."

"That dishy woman's dead?" said Isabella, horrified. She reached for the phone.

"I don't know about any dishy woman," said Alberg. "It's a man who's supposed to be dead."

Sanducci's patrol car and an ambulance were parked next to a late-model Chevrolet in the driveway behind the house. It was Sanducci who answered the door when Alberg knocked.

"The guy's her brother," he said. "He's dead, all right. Pissed out of his mind, I guess. Fell down the basement stairs."

Two ambulance attendants lounged against the wall. "Go wait in your wagon," said Alberg. "We'll call you when we need you." He said to Sanducci, "Where's the sister? Is she all right?"

"She's fine. She's in the kitchen," said Sanducci, leading the way down the hall.

She sat at the kitchen table, looking out the small, uncurtained window, her chin in her hand. She was wearing a black suit: a straight skirt, a short jacket, a white blouse with a big floppy bow at her throat.

"Miss Strachan," said Sanducci, with unusual formality, "I'd like you to meet Staff Sergeant Alberg. Staff, this is Miss Zoe Strachan."

She turned her head slightly, to look at him. Her eyes, set wide apart, were a very dark blue. She had a high, broad forehead. Her hair was black and wavy, parted at the side. Her skin was pale, and appeared to be unlined; but he knew she wasn't young. She was the most beautiful thing he'd seen since coming to Sechelt, six years before.

"Thank you, Sanducci," said Alberg.

Why hadn't he ever seen her around town?

He forced himself to look away from her, at the window. He remembered that he hadn't seen any windows to speak of in the front of the house; only a small, frosted pane that was probably a bathroom. The woman certainly liked her privacy.

"May I sit down?" he said, and Zoe Strachan nodded.

"Would you give me his full name, please." He pulled out his notebook and a pen.

"Benjamin Henry Strachan," she said.

"And he's your brother?"

"Yes."

He wrote these things in his notebook. His hands felt cold. Again he looked at the small kitchen window, through which he could see only the darkening sky. There was a lot to be said for views, he thought distractedly. He liked the one from his sunporch, for instance—down the hill to Gibsons and the harbor. But the most important thing about windows was that they let in light. He couldn't imagine living in a house that didn't let in any light down one whole side of it.

Zoe Strachan was waiting patiently, expecting more questions.

"Did he live here? On the peninsula?"

"He lived in West Vancouver."

"Was he married? Did he have a family?"

"He used to be married. Twice. The first one divorced him. The second one died."

"Any children?"

"No."

"She's his only living relative, Staff," said Sanducci. Alberg jumped slightly; he'd forgotten the corporal was there.

Zoe raised her eyes to Sanducci and gave him a tremulous smile. "Yes," she said, nodding. "I am."

"Corporal," said Alberg. "Let me know when Dr. Gillingham gets here." He waited until Sanducci had left the room.

"Your parents are dead?"

"Yes."

"What happened to them?"

She looked annoyed. Alberg didn't blame her. What the hell difference did it make, what had happened to her parents?

"My father died of a heart attack," she said, "when I was twenty-three. My mother got cancer seven years later. She was ill for a year or so and then died."

"Were you and your brother close?"

"Heavens no. We had nothing in common. Absolutely nothing at all."

"Except your parents," said Alberg.

She looked at him straight on then, and he realized that she hadn't done so before. Her head had always been turned away, or at least slightly averted. He didn't think he'd been consciously aware of that. Until now. Her gaze struck him with an almost physical force.

"Do you want to see him?" she said. "My brother?"

"Uh, yes," said Alberg. "In a minute."

"We can't just leave him there," she said thoughtfully.

"No. When the doctor's been here, your brother will be taken to—well, he'll be taken wherever you like."

He thought she smiled a little.

"I guess a funeral home," she said.

He glanced around the kitchen. In the corner, a television set sat on a small table. A large number of electric appliances were lined up, gleaming, on the countertops. An unopened bottle of red wine sat next to a toaster oven. The room was meticulously clean. Even the stainless-steel sink shone.

Zoe Strachan swiveled around on her chair and crossed her legs. Alberg couldn't remember the last time he'd heard that sound: the slithery, silken sound of stockinged legs, stroking. Women hardly ever wore stockings anymore. Even when they did, it wasn't stockings they wore but pantyhose. They hardly ever wore skirts anymore, for that matter. And they practically never wore suits. It was possible, he thought, that since she was wearing a skirt, a whole suit, in fact, and stockings, too, that possibly, just possibly, they were real stockings, not pantyhose, which meant that she'd be wearing something to hold them up, too, something like a black garter belt, maybe.

He cleared his throat and fumbled with his notebook, attempting to turn the page. His pen fell to the floor. Zoe Strachan didn't move when he reached down to retrieve it, even though it had landed right next to her foot. Alberg felt the smooth leather of her black shoe against the side of his hand as he picked up the pen.

She was looking at him curiously. He had absolutely no idea how old she was. He could see, now, that there were shimmerings of silver in her black hair. But her face was unlined, and her body was slim, even athletic.

"Corporal Sanducci suggested that your brother might have been drinking," he said.

"I'm afraid he was," said Zoe. "I think that Benjamin probably drank rather a lot."

"Tell me what happened."

"We were in the living room," she said, and stood up. Automatically, Alberg stood up, too. She was about the same height as Cassandra, he thought. No, shorter, because she was wearing high heels. "I'll show you," said Zoe, and he followed her out of the kitchen.

In the living room, she pointed to a black leather chair. "He was sitting there. I was on the sofa, there. He said he wanted to catch the three-thirty ferry, but I told him he was too drunk and that he'd better stay and have dinner with me." She looked toward Alberg, standing next to the archway leading to the hall. "He didn't get drunk here, Staff Sergeant. He was drunk when he arrived." She waited while Alberg scribbled dutifully in his notebook.

"I hadn't done my shopping for the week, though," she went on. "I told Benjamin to lie down and sleep while I went out to get something for us to eat." She sat on the sofa, resting her left arm along its low back and crossing her legs. "He agreed. But first, he said, he'd go downstairs and fetch a bottle of wine to have with dinner." She shrugged. "There's no point arguing with people when they're in that condition. So I just sat here and waited for him to come back. A few minutes later, I heard a yelp, and a crash."

She got up and walked toward Alberg. "I went to the basement door," she said, passing him, going along the hall. "It was open, just as you see it now." She stood in the doorway, looking down. "I think I called him a couple of times. It was very dark down there. I switched on the light, and there he was." She turned to Alberg with a smile. "And there he still is," she said, gesturing.

Alberg peered into the basement.

"Poor Benjamin," said Zoe.

"Why had he come to see you?"

"To borrow money," she said, continuing to gaze down the stairs.

"A lot of money?"

"I have no idea." She leaned against the doorframe, looking up at Alberg. "There wasn't any point in discussing how much he wanted, when I wasn't about to give him anything at all."

"Was he in some kind of trouble?"

"I don't think so. He didn't have enough money, that's all. Benjamin never had enough money."

"Did he have a job?"

She sighed and went back down the hall toward the kitchen, talking to Alberg over her shoulder. "Apparently he did, yes. I don't know where. As I told you, we weren't close, Benjamin and I. The only times I saw him were when he needed money." She took a coffee canister from the cupboard. "I don't know why he kept trying. I never gave him anything, and he must have known that I never would."

"Dr. Gillingham's here," said Sanducci from the doorway.

"Why don't you stay here, Miss Strachan," said Alberg.

"Yes," said Zoe, smiling. She gestured with the canister. "I'll make some coffee."

Alberg found the doctor at the bottom of the basement stairs, black bag in hand, gazing with satisfaction upon the inert form of Benjamin Henry Strachan. "Here's another one that age'll never wither, then," he said approvingly.

"Good Christ, Alex, keep your voice down," said Alberg. "His sister's upstairs."

The doctor, a swarthy man in his fifties, tried to squat down next to the corpse. "Shit, forgot the damn knee," he said. "Bring me a damn chair, will you?"

Alberg looked around the basement. He saw three doors, all closed, and opened the first one; the small room that was revealed apparently functioned as a wine cellar. In the corner was a small stool. He carried it over to Alex Gillingham. "What's wrong with your knee?"

"I twisted it. Mountain climbing."

"Christ," said Alberg.

"You oughtn't to scoff," said the doctor reproachfully. He bent over Benjamin Strachan. "You're putting on weight; I notice it more every time I see you, Karl. A little mountain climbing wouldn't do you any harm."

"Get a move on, will you? His sister wants to get the body out of here."

"Yes. I do," said Zoe from the top of the stairs.

The men looked up. She stood, motionless, with one hand on either side of the doorway, a little higher than her shoulders. One knee was flexed, the other straight. Her face was in shadow. She seemed to fill the doorway, although Alberg knew this was a trick of perspective.

He waited anxiously for her to speak again.

He wanted to move, to say something to encourage her, but he was transfixed.

"Well," said the doctor. He nudged Alberg. "I can certainly understand that, ma'am. And you can be assured that I'm going to get this matter dealt with just as quickly as I can." He nudged Alberg again. "Get up there, Staff Sergeant, and keep the lady amused."

At the top of the stairs, Zoe laughed.

CHAPTER

21

Ramona had looked around her on Thursday afternoon and seen the plants and known that left alone for three weeks, some of them were going to die. She knew then that Marcia must have left her key with someone who'd agreed to come in and water them. That somebody was bound to be Marcia's mother, Reba McLean. Ramona figured that was how the policeman had gotten in; he'd borrowed the key from Reba McLean.

So she could expect Reba to come clattering up to the door any old time now, driving that beat-up white Beetle she tootled around in. Ramona knew she couldn't be here when that happened. Reba knew the house too well. She'd spot the slightest thing that looked different; out of place. And she'd poke around, too, making herself right at home, maybe even peering into the back of the closet.

Ramona tried and tried, that night and during the next day,

to think of where she might go. She was very worried, very anxious.

And she didn't like to admit it to herself, but there wasn't any point in trying to deny it: sometime Friday afternoon she lost some more time. When she "came to," she was huddled in the back of the bedroom closet again. That relieved her mind somewhat: to know that she apparently had the wit, even while witless, to remember that she was in hiding.

She'd lost time while she was in the hospital, too; but it hadn't mattered so much there.

Now it was Saturday morning. Ramona once more checked the soil in the plant pots. None was completely dried out yet, but most of them were due for a watering, all right.

She wondered what Anton would have had to say about her predicament, and that brought a smile to her face, which made her feel a little better. She sat down at the rickety kitchen table with a pencil and a pad of lined yellow paper, and she started making lists.

First she put down the good things about her situation. Although her mind certainly did meander off somewhere periodically, she thought that when in attendance, it was brighter and brisker than it had been for some time. Physically, she was feeling a whole lot better than she had any right to feel.

But on the other side of the ledger, she had to leave her house, and that was a sorry blow. Today she had to do a reconnaissance, try to find a house farther along the beach that was unlocked and temporarily unoccupied.

Another minus—she had to admit it—she was going to get bored and restless, eventually. At the moment she was entirely enjoying the freedom to do whatever she wanted, whenever she wanted to do it. But she knew that after a certain number of days—she had no idea how many—her craving for companionship would reassert itself. Would she have to go back to the hospital, then?

Ramona knew Dr. Gillingham hadn't persuaded her into that place because he wanted her to be miserable. He'd truly believed that she wasn't capable of looking after herself properly.

Maybe not permanently, she thought. But temporarily, at least, I can do it. Temporarily, at least, I want to be on my own again.

She wrote these things down, and studied them.

Well, her way was plainly laid out for her. She was going to enjoy every second of her freedom, however long it lasted.

She might have to confide in a friend, eventually. When she ran out of clothes, or of books to read, or got sick of her own company.

But she wasn't ready to do that yet.

First order of business—locate another burrow. And find another food supply.

She pushed her chair away from the table and got up, stiffly. She'd better decide what to take with her.

Into the shopping bag she loaded some extra pairs of socks, from Robbie's bureau drawer. A pair of Marcia's slacks. A roll of toilet paper. The bottle of gin. The pad of paper on which she'd made her lists. And the pencil.

That was about as much as she could comfortably lug around, she figured.

While she struggled to get the tweed coat on over her three sweaters, she recalled the commotion she'd observed the day before at the Strachan woman's place. Ramona had seen at least one police car head up the driveway, and then an ambulance had arrived. She wondered if the poor woman had been taken ill.

She'd just put her hand on the doorknob when she heard a car pull up on the gravel verge of the road, in front of the house.

She turned swiftly around and grabbed the shopping bag, to take it into the closet with her.

She heard a car door slam shut. Two people were coming. She heard them talking, she heard a woman talking to a man, and the man saying "Uh huh."

Reba.

Ramona looked frantically around the house.

Then she opened the door and fled through a break in the hedge into the Ferrises' yard, and from there she hightailed it up to the road, and eventually down again, onto the beach.

She lurched furtively along the beach, feeling like that convict—she couldn't remember his name—feeling like that convict in *Great Expectations*.

She'd forgotten to bring the tuque she'd been using.

She'd forgotten her gloves, too; and her scarf.

Ramona stumbled along the sand, dazed and anxious, clutching her shopping bag.

C H A P T E R

22

Zoe didn't want to move. She was vehement about this. But in the end she had no choice.

She put up an awful fuss. She cried and screamed and banged her heels. She knew she was behaving like an infant, but she didn't know what else to do. She was horrified, full of dread; she could not believe that it was actually going to happen.

Her parents were upset and worried by her conduct, but they didn't even consider changing their minds. When she realized that no matter what she did, it wasn't even going to occur to them not to do this awful thing, she stopped crying and screaming and banging her heels.

She was sullen and resentful for a long time. They kept trying to coax her out of it. For months before the move they talked to her enthusiastically about their new house, which was in West Vancouver, next to the ocean. They even drove her there, but she stayed in the car, staring out the window at the street. She wouldn't even look at the new house.

She had nightmares about dying, about having no breath, about people coming after her, brandishing knives.

Her father drew careful diagrams of the rooms in the new house and asked her opinion about what furniture should go where. But Zoe refused to participate. Her father said she was to get first choice among the bedrooms; in the old house Benjamin had had first choice, because he'd been born first. But Zoe didn't care which bedroom she got. Her father said he'd take her to the two high schools that served the area where they were going to live, so that she could decide which she liked better. But Zoe wouldn't go with him.

Sometimes she made an effort to imagine living in a different house. But she was alarmed at the way that felt: it made her have more nightmares.

She was furious not to be able to make up her own mind about such an important thing as where she was to live.

The months passed, and eventually the school year was over and it was time to move. At first Zoe refused to pack her own belongings, but her mother got sharp with her and said that unless she did it herself, Benjamin would be dispatched to do it for her. So she packed up the things in her bedroom while Benjamin watched her, snickering, from the hallway, until Zoe finally slammed the door on him.

On the day of the move, Zoe left the house early in the morning and stayed away all day.

When she returned, the movers had come and gone. Benjamin and her parents were eating sandwiches at the picnic table in the backyard; the new house didn't have a backyard, so they were leaving the picnic table behind. Her father pushed the plate of sandwiches across the table to Zoe.

"I'm not hungry," she said.

Her father rubbed the side of his head; he had quite a lot of gray in his hair now.

"*Okay,*" *he said quietly.* "*Then let's go.*"

And they got in the car and drove to West Vancouver, about fifty miles away.

They stayed in a hotel that night.

The next morning they met the movers at the new house. Late that day they discovered that three boxes were missing, two boxes of Zoe's parents' books and one box of Zoe's things. Her father asked her to make a list of what she thought was in it, for insurance or something, but Zoe didn't know what was in it. She'd just tossed things in until a box was full, closed it, taped it, opened another box, tossed things in until it was full, and on and on.

She left most of her unpacking for weeks and weeks, until the end of the summer approached, and Benjamin got back from working at the Great North mine, and Zoe had to get ready to go to a new school. When everything was finally hauled out of boxes and put away, she realized that some of her old scribblers had been in the box of stuff that got lost.

It was time she got rid of them anyway, she thought, and she tore up the rest of them and burned them in the fireplace.

CHAPTER
23

On Saturday morning in Alberg's office, Sokolowski reported gloomily, "Her kids are on the phone to me half a dozen times a day."

"Why aren't they here helping us look for her, that's what I'd like to know," said Isabella. She was leaning against the wall, with her arms crossed.

"The son, Horatio, or whatever his name is . . ." The sergeant began thumbing through his notebook.

"Horace," said Isabella.

"Yeah, Horace. He wants to know how long does she have to be missing before she's legally dead."

"Christ," said Alberg.

"Yeah." Sokolowski turned to Isabella. "She's Spanish, right?"

"Who? Ramona? Spanish?"

"Yeah. Ramona. That's a Spanish name."

Isabella was shaking her head. "She's not Spanish."

"Yeah?" Sokolowski looked exceedingly disappointed. "You sure?"

"She's not Spanish."

"So we've got nothing but dead ends, right?" said Alberg.

"Right, Staff. It wasn't her on the bus to Powell River. It wasn't her hitchhiking out by Porpoise Bay. It wasn't her on the ferry. She hasn't showed up at the liquor store. She's disappeared into thin air." He uttered the phrase as though it were newly minted.

"I think—can I tell you what I think?" said Isabella to Alberg.

"Go ahead."

"I think you should have another look in her house."

"She isn't there, Isabella," said Sokolowski. "I assure you."

"Maybe she was hiding under the bed."

"Oh, sure, a seventy-five-year-old lady, she's gonna hide herself underneath a bed."

"Maybe not under the bed, okay," said Isabella. "But if she was there in the house, she sure wouldn't want you to find her. So she'd be hiding, all right."

Today Isabella was wearing over a white shirt and a brown T-shirt a brown-and-white sweater that looked to Alberg vaguely Icelandic in design. He wondered if she'd knitted it herself. It was awfully big. But Isabella liked her sweaters big.

"You could go take another look, Sid," he said. "It wouldn't hurt."

"Yeah," said Sokolowski reluctantly.

"She can't get at any money, the lawyer says," said Alberg. "So how's she eating?"

"She might be staying with someone," said Isabella hopefully. "You know. A friend."

Alberg gazed at her. "If she'd gone to you, Isabella, and said she didn't want anybody to know where she was, would you have taken her in and looked after her and kept it a secret?"

"I couldn't have," said Isabella sorrowfully. "Not with my hubby and my Jimmy around."

"If you were on your own, though."

Isabella tilted her head and looked thoughtfully toward the ceiling. "I would have," she said after a minute.

"Great," said Sokolowski. "Terrific." He lumbered out of the chair. "I'll phone Reba McLean." He sighed. "I hate this kind of thing."

"She's going to turn up," said Isabella firmly.

Sokolowski left the room, shaking his head.

"So tell me," said Isabella to Alberg, "is she as dishy as they say?"

"Who?" said Alberg, pretending to glance at his watch.

"The Strachan woman. Whose brother got drunk and fell down her basement stairs, thereby killing himself."

"You seem to know an awful lot about it," said Alberg, nettled.

"Sanducci told me. He's going around looking like some-body hit him on the head with a hammer. So tell me," she said. "She's a real knockout, eh?"

"Sanducci. Christ. She's old enough to be his mother."

Isabella frowned, uncertain.

"His aunt, then. Haven't you got things to do?"

"I knew it," said Isabella with satisfaction. "Somebody told me she used to be an actress."

"I've got to be out of here in less than an hour," said Alberg. "Go away."

"Or maybe it was a model."

"Isabella. Beat it."

"Probably no truth to it, though. People can be gorgeous,

after all, and not be models. What do you think she does for a living?"

Alberg got up and held open his office door. "Goodbye, Isabella."

His phone rang. It was Alex Gillingham.

"Alex. So what's the word?"

"Pain," said Gillingham, and broke into a cackle.

Alex Gillingham was always in a state of injury. The knee that had been bothering him at Zoe Strachan's house was just the most recent in a continuous stream of complaints, some more serious than others.

He had become addicted to sport. Sometimes he limped, with a wonky ankle. Sometimes his shoulder bothered him. And sometimes his distress was more generalized. "Ah, the old bones hurt," he would confide to Alberg. "Been overdoing it again, I guess." He'd say this with satisfaction. His aim, apparently, was to relentlessly batter his body into a dazed insensitivity to pain—and therefore, maybe, to disease, as well.

"Strachan," said Alberg patiently. "What's the word on Benjamin Strachan."

"Died of a broken neck. Bet you didn't even need me to tell you that, did you? But I'm not done with him yet. There's a couple of things that are kinda funny."

"Oh yeah? Funny how?"

Gillingham had been on call to the RCMP for about a year. Sometimes he feigned exasperation about being called away from whatever he was doing to attend the scene of a death, but Alberg knew this for the sham it was. The doctor hardly ever left the peninsula, because he was afraid he might miss something. Alberg was convinced that if Gillingham were dealing with a patient in extremis and suddenly got summoned by the RCMP, the patient would be shit out of luck.

"And make it quick," the staff sergeant added. "I've got a plane to catch."

"He's got a crack on the back of his head."

"Yeah, well, he fell down the stairs, didn't he. I'm not surprised he hit his head."

"Hmm. Not the right kind of wound, though."

Two winters ago, Gillingham had taken up skiing. The following summer, windsurfing. And now it was hiking. Except that he called it mountain climbing. He had no patience for things like tennis, racquetball, or squash. They were competitive and therefore largely intellectual pursuits, he maintained. He preferred, as he put it, "to pit myself against nature herself." But he hurled himself against her with such ardor, attacked her with such force, that Alberg thought it no wonder that nature perceived him as berserk and routinely punished him.

He had not been like this when Alberg first met him. Only for the last two years or so; since he'd left his wife. He was the only man Alberg knew who left his marriage not for another woman but for an apocalyptic but fundamentally unsatisfying affair with Mother Nature.

"What do you mean," said Alberg, "it's not the right kind of wound?"

"Just what I said. And there's a big jeezly bruise on his stomach, too."

"What are you trying to tell me?"

"I don't know, Karl. Maybe nothing. But it feels kinda weird, you know what I mean?"

"Alex," said Alberg wearily. "The man fell down a flight

of stairs, broke his neck, and died. Sign the form, will you?"

"Granted, he went down the stairs," said Gillingham, "and granted, his neck broke, and granted, he died. But there's this crack on the head, too. And this bruise on the stomach. All conspiring to puzzle me some."

Alberg realized that he was feeling cold, and anxious, and he wondered if he was getting the flu. "I'm going to miss my plane," he muttered, "if I'm not careful."

"I can't say that he fell down those stairs," said Gillingham. "How the hell do I know that he fell? I wasn't there. Were you?"

"It's fair to make an assumption here, for God's sake," Alberg shouted into the phone. "The man is lying on a concrete floor at the bottom of the damn stairs; and he's got a broken neck. It's fair to assume, Alex, that the trip down the stairs is what caused the broken neck. Why do you have a problem with that? What the hell *is* your problem, anyway?" He was astonished by his anger.

"Maybe he didn't fall," said Gillingham quietly. "That's my problem. In a nutshell."

Alberg suddenly remembered the keys. Zoe Strachan had wanted her brother's car removed from her driveway. Alberg offered to have it taken to the detachment parking lot. But he hadn't been able to find any keys on Benjamin Strachan's body. It turned out that Zoe had them.

She'd explained that, of course. "I took them away from him," she said, detaching the car keys from her brother's key ring. "I didn't want him to even think about driving when he was drunk." She'd handed the car keys to Alberg, smiling, and put the key ring back in her purse.

"Do your job, Alex," said Alberg quietly. "Sign the damn form." He hung up.

Alberg sat still at his desk, thinking.

She aroused in him a thrill of dread that he couldn't explain, and had no wish to investigate.

There was no reason she shouldn't have had Benjamin Strachan's keys.

It was the wine bottle on the kitchen counter that suddenly bothered him.

CHAPTER

24

By the time Alberg and Gillingham had departed and Benjamin's body had been removed, the last ferry had left Langdale for Horseshoe Bay. So Zoe had to wait until Saturday morning to set out for West Vancouver.

In the cafeteria she recognized several faces: a woman who worked as a checkout cashier at the Super-Valu, another who performed the same function at London Drugs, the man who owned the hardware store.

She didn't notice Karl Alberg.

Alberg was on the ship-to-shore phone when he saw her. He was talking with Cassandra. He saw Zoe Strachan, and the words in his mouth dissolved.

"Karl. Karl?" said Cassandra.

Zoe was sitting by the window, sipping every so often from a Styrofoam cup.

She found the view unutterably depressing. Gray skies and sullen seas didn't usually bother her, but on this gloomy

116

morning she found herself wishing for sunshine. The mainland seemed to loom threateningly against the horizon; the channel they were crossing felt to Zoe in a state of disorder—lumpy islands strewn sloppily about, no rhyme or reason to their disposition among the waters of Howe Sound; she could easily believe that they habitually changed their positions, just to be perverse.

Alberg couldn't imagine her pitching her brother down the stairs.

"Karl, are you there or not?" said Cassandra.

"Yeah, sorry, I'm here. Listen. I've gotta go. I'll be back late Monday; I'll call you then. Say hi to your mother for me." He hung up and strolled casually over to the rack of tourism pamphlets near the entrance to the stairway that led down to the car decks.

He wondered where she was going, and why. It must have something to do with making funeral arrangements. Maybe she was going to her brother's place of work, he thought, to break the news of his death in person. But then he remembered it was Saturday. And besides, she'd said she didn't know where he worked.

Her black hair swung toward her face as she bent to take a sip of coffee. She looked up suddenly, and Alberg thought she had spotted him—it was ludicrous, he felt like a bloody idiot, but when she turned her face toward him his heart started to pound. Then she looked away, out the window again.

Zoe watched various craft stitch their way across the water: a small tug towing a log boom, a fishing boat heading in to shore, a sailboat, motoring, with sails furled. They were close to Horseshoe Bay now. Another ferry passed, on its way to Nanaimo, and the Bowen Island ferry, too, much smaller; it looked as if it was chewing its way through the water, small and ferocious, spewing foam from the sides of its mouth.

Alberg, ostensibly engrossed in some literature about Butchart Gardens, studied her intently. Surveillance, he told himself. But he didn't feel like a police officer. He felt like a voyeur.

Zoe was cautiously congratulating herself. She thought she had handled things rather well, under the circumstances. She'd forgotten about the damned wine bottle, sitting on the hall floor, but had managed to move it into the kitchen without the corporal noticing. And the other one, the staff sergeant, had been perfectly willing to accept that she had separated Benjamin from his keys because he'd been drunk.

Zoe just wanted to get on with it, to find the damn scribblers, burn them, and settle back into her life. They weren't in his car, which meant they had to be in the house, or in his office, or in a safe-deposit box in a bank somewhere. But the house, she thought, the house was the most likely place.

She looked up again, toward the bow, toward Alberg. "Jesus," he muttered under his breath. Her skin, her hair, her eyes . . . He watched her stand up and sling her big leather bag over her shoulder, moving in jeans and boots and denim jacket with grace and sensuality.

And then he looked again into her face.

With a terrible coldness gathering in the center of him, he identified what made Zoe Strachan extraordinary. It was not the way she looked. It was not haughtiness, or remoteness, or unattentiveness. It was not the presence of anything; it was an absence.

Something was missing from Zoe Strachan. He was extremely reluctant to consider what it might be.

CHAPTER

25

Ramona clambered up the incline onto the Strachan woman's property, hauling her shopping bag, and leaned once more upon the massive Douglas fir, to catch her breath and plan her strategy.

Yes, she was certain of it, there was only one explanation for that ambulance showing up. The poor woman must have been taken ill—maybe it was appendicitis—and they'd whisked her off to the hospital.

And she lived alone, the whole town knew that. Therefore her house would be vacant.

This was so clear to Ramona that she had begun to think she actually recalled having a telephone conversation with Dr. Gillingham about it. The Strachan woman is worried about leaving her house empty, he might have said, and I've told her that you're looking for a place to stay, temporarily, how would you feel about house-sitting for her?

Ramona, resting against the fir tree, imagined herself as a

professional house-sitter, moving from one place to another, tending people's homes in exchange for food and lodging.

Cautiously, she moved from the shelter of the trees onto the driveway, and headed toward the house.

She was very nervous as she crept along. It was possible that she was wrong. The Strachan woman might be perfectly healthy, and inhabiting her house as usual. If that was the case, she was apt to appear right in front of Ramona at any second, out for another jog, or ready to drive into town for groceries or whatever. Well if that happened Ramona would pretend to be lost, that's all.

She shifted the shopping bag from her right hand to her left and pushed her hair away from her forehead; her hair was a mess, far too long, and sloppy-looking, with the perm clinging just to the ends of it. She knew she looked a sight. She had been scrupulous about rinsing out her underwear and her knee-highs every night, so what she wore next to her skin was always clean. But her dress was grimy, and her socks, and the sweaters she'd borrowed from Marcia, they were all badly in need of a wash.

The shopping bag was getting heavy.

She crunched reluctantly along the gravel, wishing that the sun were shining. It wasn't the friendliest place around, this promontory, sticking out into the sea like a great rude thumb. She could do with a bit of bright sunshine to perk up her spirits, give her some courage.

The ocean was doing a lot of crashing around, out behind the house; there would be rocks there, then, instead of sand.

Ramona ambled along more and more slowly, but she was only putting off the inevitable; unless she started walking backward, she was going to get there sooner or later.

And then there she was, standing right beside the house, looking at the door.

The ocean was making a whole lot of noise, and the arbutus trees that were clustered around the house scrabbled at the roof like fingernails against a blackboard.

As she lifted her hand she had a sense that she hadn't thought this through . . . she wasn't altogether sure what she was doing there . . . why she was feeling so nervous? . . . but she rang the bell.

Who lived here, anyway? thought Ramona, her heart starting to pound.

Nobody. Or else they were out.

The Strachan woman, that's who lived here.

In a rush, clarity returned: Thank you, God, thought Ramona; but she kept on being frightened, feeling threatened.

I'll pretend to be lost, she thought, if she comes to the door. There's absolutely nothing to be nervous about, nothing at all, she told herself, but her heart was going a mile a minute, which she knew wasn't good for it, and there was a shaking in her knees that was making it harder and harder for her to stand up.

She realized that nobody was responding to the bell.

With somewhat more boldness, she rang it again.

And again.

Nobody home. Definitely.

Hopefully, she tried the door. But it was locked.

She decided to go around the house and see if she could get in through a window.

But first she had a look in the garage . . . and the garage was empty.

Ramona realized there was no point in trying to get into the house, because if the Strachan woman was out somewhere in her car, then she certainly wasn't laid up in the hospital.

And she was liable to come driving up her driveway here any minute now.

Ramona scurried away from the house, the shopping bag banging against her ankle.

She was about halfway to the road when she heard the sound of whistling and saw a figure turn into the driveway. She straightaway flung herself into the brush and hid behind a tree and watched as Sandy McAllister traipsed past, his mailbag slung over his shoulder. She had to clamp her hand over her mouth to prevent herself from calling out to him; she'd been on his route, when she lived in her house, and he'd often had coffee with her on cold winter mornings. She watched while he delivered the mail, passed her again, and disappeared around the corner where the driveway met the road.

Ramona, hiding in the woods, considered her situation. Things weren't going well anymore. She didn't feel good in her body. And she was uncertain, depressed; her mind felt all cobwebby.

Maybe she ought to call Isabella. Or Rosie. Or even Dr. Gillingham.

This was a bleak prospect, but comforting, too. People would look after her. Wash her clothes. Arrange for her to get a perm. Talk to her.

And put her back in the hospital.

Ramona realized she was looking directly at what appeared to be a tiny house. It was tucked among the trees about thirty feet in from the driveway, on the opposite side. There was a small window to the right of the door, but the curtains were drawn. It had a forlorn, abandoned look. She almost hadn't seen it, it was so hidden by trees and brush.

Ramona hobbled across the driveway. She tried the door, but it was locked. She began to be annoyed with that Strachan woman, where did she think she was living, anyway, New York City? All her damn doors locked.

Ramona made her way around the little house, which was encircled by a well-worn path, and at the back was another door. This one had a window in the top half of it.

And the window was broken. Shreds of bark stuck to the broken glass, and a tree branch sprawled beneath it, on the porch. Ramona looked up into the thick, dense branches of a cedar tree. It was making soft, whispering sounds.

She put down the shopping bag. Carefully, she reached through the window and down, and fumbled around until she found the doorknob, which turned easily, and the little lock thing in the middle popped right out. There was a chain lock, too, so she had to slide the bolt out, and she did that, and then the door was open.

Ramona stepped back, amazed.

She felt positively merry, all of a sudden.

God's in his heaven, Ramona chortled to herself. All's right with the world.

Then she picked up the shopping bag and went through the door and into Zoe Strachan's cottage.

CHAPTER

26

In West Vancouver, Zoe parked her car in a small paved lot that served three or four houses located below the road. She noticed that a fence had been erected, but it wasn't a tall one. She could have toppled him over it, all right. She took hold of the top railing and looked down. The cliff was about fifty feet high; the house was built halfway down, wedged into sheer rock. There was a steep flight of steps down to the front door, and another, which couldn't be seen from the road, that led from the back of the house all the way down to a rocky beach. Zoe's father had kept a small boat there, for puttering about in. Benjamin used to like to go fishing in it.

There was also an elevator, installed after Zoe left home. It was a cage with a locked door. She got Benjamin's key ring from her purse and found the key that fit. The elevator delivered her slowly, smoothly, but noisily to the house. She got out, closed the cage door, and found the house keys. She unlocked the door and stepped inside.

There was a strange hush upon the place. Zoe stood still and listened intently to the silence, which was like sudden silence after clamor; it had an echo affixed to it.

She was in a wide foyer bathed in filtered light from a translucent skylight and panels of stained glass on either side of the front door. It looked different from when she had lived in the house. Eventually she remembered that the floor had been made of oak and kept highly polished, with a few small rugs scattered about in deference to wet shoes. Now there was tile beneath her feet, in a Mediterranean pattern of some kind; Zoe wondered with distaste if the whole house had been redone in ersatz Spanish.

She moved from the foyer toward the living room . . . and stopped in the hallway, frowning. She heard nothing. But she fancied that she felt something, a current of something, somewhere in the house. She shook her head impatiently. This was no time to start imagining things.

In the living room she was astonished to find no furniture at all, just bunches of huge pillows in various brilliant colors stacked here and there. The floor in this room was still oak, but it was scratched and dull. She crossed to the windows that looked out and down, down, down toward the beach, hidden from view by an outcrop of rock. At the sides of the house arbutus trees clung to the cliffside, their branches brushing the roof. Zoe threw open the windows and heard the muffled soughing of the sea and the idle scribbling of the arbutus branches against shingles; the same sounds she heard at home, but different.

She didn't want to be in this house. She wanted to be back in her own living room, looking out upon her own austere patio.

She pulled the windows closed and locked them.

Where on earth can the furniture be? she wondered, staring at the bare room. Bare floors, bare walls—she decided that Benjamin must have stripped the place, sold everything.

Now she did hear something. A soft shuffling sound. She was certain of it.

She tried to think what could possibly have caused it. Perhaps Benjamin owned some kind of pet, a dog or a cat. She listened hard, concentrating, hardly breathing.

Nothing.

Perhaps it was only the sound of the sea, made more distant now that she'd closed the window. She moved as silently as possible from the living room, trying to prevent her boots from clicking on the wooden floor.

At the end of the hall she found the master bedroom, once occupied by her parents. Beneath a pair of uncurtained corner windows that looked through arbutus branches at the sky was a huge bathtub. Astonished, Zoe gazed at it, remembering the small desk that used to be tucked into that corner. Her mother had sat there to do the household accounts. The bathtub was enormous, with a wide ledge. There were jets installed inside it.

The bedroom floor was carpeted, except for a tiled area around the tub, and there was a tacky white wicker shelf unit stacked with towels leaning against the wall. The bed was immense, at least king-sized, and unmade, the bedspread tossed to the floor, the sheets, the quilt, and four outsize pillows rumpled; Zoe crinkled her nose and sniffed the air. She wondered how long it had been since the sheets were changed. She wondered what Benjamin had done about sex, when he no longer had a wife handy. She tried to imagine him prowling the bars, making his mind up, taking his pick; she tried to imagine him anonymous and predatory, but she couldn't; it was preposterous. She laughed, thinking about this—and heard a scurrying sound from the hall.

She strode to the door and looked out, but saw nothing. Everything was quiet. "Here, kitty, kitty, kitty," she said irritably. Zoe loathed cats. They made her skin crawl. "Here, kitty, kitty, kitty." But no cat appeared. Zoe heard nothing more.

She stood there indecisively. The house was making her uneasy. She was positively rattled. She didn't care for this at all.

Cautiously she pushed open the door to the room next to the master bedroom, the room that had once been hers. From the hallway she peered inside. Benjamin had obviously been using it as an office. She looked in at filing cabinets and bookcases and a large desk; and she was absolutely certain that somewhere in this room he had hidden the scribblers.

She had just stepped into the room when she heard a noise so indisputably real that the hair stood up on the back of her neck. She whirled around, heart pounding.

"My God," said Zoe. "Who are you?"

He was sitting on the floor, his back against the wall. His eyes were wild and his knees were drawn up and his small hands, in fists, were pressed against his mouth.

"I said, who are you?" said Zoe, loudly.

His clothes were a mess. He'd been crying. His face was filthy.

"What are you doing here, you wretched little trespasser?" said Zoe.

He scuttled along the floor like a crab, toward the door.

"Oh no you don't, young man," said Zoe, and reached out to slam the door shut. "You aren't going anywhere, until you tell me what you're doing in this house."

"I live here!" cried the boy.

C H A P T E R

27

Alberg rented a car at the Calgary airport. Maura had said she would pick him up and squire him around, but he wanted none of that: he needed to have his own transportation.

Diana had made reservations for him at a motel near the campus, and Janey had written him a letter with meticulous directions as to how to get there.

It was a frigid, sullen day, he noticed, making his way along Sixteenth Avenue. The sky looked as though it were made of cast iron. And there was a wind cold enough to freeze the balls off a brass monkey.

In his motel room he found everything he wanted: a queen-sized bed, a big television set, and a bathroom with a tub and a shower. He put down the bag and checked out the TV. Not perfect, but it would do. He left it on and had just stretched out on the bed, hands behind his head, when the phone rang.

"Pops, you're there!" said Diana. "Why didn't you call?"

"I just got here," he protested. "I practically just walked in the door."

"Well, is it okay? The place?"

"Oh, yeah, it's fine," he said, turning off the television set with the remote control device. "Perfect. Everything I need."

"Good. Listen. The three of us are spending tomorrow together, right? You, me, and Janey?"

"Right," said Alberg, smiling.

"So we thought that tonight, maybe we could all of us go out for dinner. We figured to get as many free meals out of you as possible, while you're here."

"Sounds good to me," he said. "But I'd better call your mom first, just to say hello. How about if I pick you up in an hour? Give me directions," he said, switching the phone to his left hand so he could fumble in his jacket pocket for pen and paper. "And then we'll go get Janey. I better call her, too."

"Pop. Stop making decisions. Listen."

"Yeah. What?"

"I'm calling from Grandma and Grandpa's place. Janey's here, too. So is Mom. I meant how about if we *all* go out for dinner?"

"You mean your mom, too?"

"And Grandma and Grandpa. Everybody. Please?"

"Shit."

"Pop."

"Yeah. Shit. Okay."

"Thanks, Pop. I love you."

"Yeah. I know it."

He hung up the phone and stared at his suitcase. He'd brought one good jacket and one good pair of pants. They were for Monday. And some cords and a polo shirt. They were for tomorrow. What the hell was he going to wear tonight?

He unzipped the case and hauled out his good clothes and hung them up. There were a few creases, but he thought they'd probably disappear overnight. He also hung up the polo shirt and the cords and put his good shoes on the floor of the closet. He put his shaving kit in the bathroom and a paperback copy of Tom Wolfe's *The Bonfire of the Vanities* on one of the bedside tables. The presents he'd brought for his daughters went on top of the desk. He left his clean underwear and socks in the suitcase and set it on one of the room's two chairs.

He looked at his watch, and placed a call to Sechelt.

"Just checking in," he said to Sid Sokolowski.

"You've only been gone about four hours, Staff."

"Yeah, well, I wondered if Gillingham's sent over his report yet. On the Strachan guy's death."

"Not yet. I gotta tell you, though, now I'm talking to you. Isabella was right."

"About what?"

"I go back to the old lady's house, where she used to live. I go back there with Reba McLean. And Reba looks around, lets out a squeak, says somebody's been there."

Alberg sat down on the edge of the bed. "Yeah? How'd she know?"

"Stuff moved around. A chair, belongs in the bedroom, it's in the living room now. And listen, I know it for a fact, the damn chair was in the bedroom the first time I checked the place out."

Alberg grinned. "So maybe she *was* hiding under the bed."

Sokolowski made no response.

"Just kidding, Sid. Probably she hadn't gotten there yet."

"That's the way I figure it anyway," said the sergeant. "She likely sneaked in there later in the day. Musta had a key."

"You went through the place pretty thoroughly, I guess," said Alberg, still grinning. "Today, I mean."

"Yeah. She wasn't there. But I borrowed Reba's key and gave it to Sanducci. He's going to check the place during his shift."

"Good."

"Another thing. I talked to the neighbors again. They didn't see her, didn't hear anything. But the old couple with the dog, they figure they had a break-in. Didn't report it because the stuff that went missing, it was food, plus a bottle of gin."

Alberg laughed.

"Yeah," said Sokolowski. "I'm kinda glad she picked herself up some gin."

It was six o'clock when Alberg left the motel. There was a cold wind blowing, and he shivered as he hurried to his rented car. He was getting soft in his old age; too accustomed to the balmy winters of the Sunshine Coast.

On his way to the house of his former in-laws, it occurred to him that he should be bringing some kind of token gift— flowers, or chocolates, or something. Probably he should have something for Maura, too.

Somebody had probably written a book about it. More than one somebody, probably. And he'd bet his bottom dollar that they were all female, all these people who had written books about the etiquette of divorce which he'd never seen, never even looked for in the bookstore or in Cassandra's library. He'd ask her, when he got back. Got any books about forming altered but still meaningful relationships with your ex–in-laws?

He wondered where Zoe Strachan was at that moment.

Dressed in jeans and boots and a denim jacket. He thought that in summer she probably wore sunglasses a lot.

Were there men in her life? Had there ever been a husband in her life? There was no sign of one now. Maybe she was divorced, like him.

Alberg no longer found it painful to see his ex-wife. In fact, he looked forward to it. Their meetings created confusion in him but it was a shy kind of confusion, not unpleasant, and there was this strong familiarity, too, and a strangeness at the same time, and the mixture of the familiarity and the strangeness always made him tense and excited, as though anything could happen.

He came across a small shopping mall and discovered a flower shop there that was still open. He chose something called a gloxinia for the old folks and decided he had to get out of the shop then, because the fragrances in there were suffocating him. He'd get Maura candy, he thought. But then he wondered if she might be on a diet. Maura was naturally thin, and he'd never known her to go on a diet before, but everybody seemed to be doing it, so maybe she was, too.

He stood there, holding the damned gloxinia, looking worriedly at an African violet, and wondered what to do. He thought about buying her a kite. He saw her standing on top of a hill, the wind blowing her skirt and her hair, and she was holding on to the kite he'd given her; it was sailing high in the sky above her, and she was laughing. He stood there holding the gloxinia and looking at an African violet and tried to remember how it was that he'd gotten to be divorced.

The door opened before he got a chance to ring the bell, and there were his daughters, both of them. As soon as he saw them he felt a terrible pain in his heart that he guessed must be joy, because he certainly didn't feel sad, seeing them standing there. They were smiling and holding out their arms, and then they were hugging him; he felt their hair against his cheeks; they smelled sweet and young. He closed his eyes and let them hold him. He thought he would have been content to stand there forever, seeing nothing, protected by the encircling arms of his daughters. He realized that beneath his closed lids his eyes were watering. He blinked several times, then, shit, who cares, he thought, and looked at them defiantly, Diana and Janey; so he was their hostage, so what, he thought; and then he saw that they were crying, too.

"Oh dear, look at us," said Diana. "My God, Janey, he's brought plants. Are they for us?"

"He knows we'd kill them," said Janey. "They must be for Mom." She gave him a tender, approving smile.

"One of them is for your mom," said Alberg. "This one," he said, holding out the violet. "The other one's for your grandmother."

"Nothing for us," said Diana resignedly, and took the plants from him.

Janey took Alberg by the arm and led him inside. "Mom," she caroled, "Dad's here," and she gave him a sideways smile that he couldn't decipher.

Maura appeared at the end of the hall. She was instantly familiar to him. This happened every time he saw her, and he was always surprised. Even when something about her had changed—the way she dressed, the way she wore her hair, something about her makeup—he noted this and in the same instant felt an intimacy with her that he had never known with anyone else. Seeing her made him smile and caused his bones to ache, all at the same time.

"Hi," he said.

"Hi, Karl. Come on in. Do you want some coffee?"

She led the way into the kitchen. Behind him, his daughters danced and shuffled.

His mother-in-law sat at the kitchen table, cradling a mug of coffee between her hands. There was a magazine open on the table in front of her, and she was wearing her reading glasses. She didn't take them off, so he knew she didn't intend to stand up and give him a hug. He bent to kiss her cheek, murmuring hello, and she said, "Hello, Karl," in that limpid, melodious voice he liked so much. Her face was wrinkled and leathery; she had always loved the sun.

Alberg backed away from her and sat down. "How have you been, Peggy?"

"I've been reasonably well, Karl. And you?"

"Oh, thriving," he said, looking up at Diana and Janey. "Thriving. Well, you know. Maybe not thriving."

"Look, Grandma," said Diana, setting the gloxinia on the table. "Dad brought it. And Mom, this one's for you," she said, offering the violet.

They each said thank you, and Alberg said it was nothing.

"It's really very good to see you, Karl," said Maura, smiling at him, and Alberg smiled back, cleared his throat, stammered something—and thought suddenly, inexplicably, of Zoe Strachan, appearing, backlit, at the top of her basement stairs. Maura was wearing a gray sweater and a red-and-gray plaid skirt, and shoes with high heels. So of course she'd be wearing pantyhose, too. Or stockings. He acknowledged that it was possible she might be wearing stockings. But never, he thought, gazing at her fondly—surely, never—a black garter belt.

Then Maura's father came into the kitchen. Alberg stood up, and they shook hands.

"Pop," said Diana, "look at that. Grandpa's smaller around the waist than you are. I thought policemen were supposed to stay fit."

"I quit smoking," said Alberg feebly.

"Well, that's good," said Arthur Lobb.

"That's very good," said Maura. "How long has it been?"

"Six months."

"Well, look, the worst is over, then," said Arthur. "Or so I've heard."

"Diana smokes," said Janey. "I wish she wouldn't."

"Shut your mouth, sweetheart," said Diana.

"I hear you're taking us out for supper," said Arthur.

"Yeah," said Alberg heartily. "Where would you like to go?"

"I took the liberty," said Maura, "of making reservations."

"Ah," said Alberg.

"I hope you don't mind."

"Oh, no. Of course not." He beamed weakly at them all, struggling for equilibrium against a sudden and powerful attack of déjà-vu.

C H A P T E R

28

There was a bidet in the bathroom.

Ramona hadn't seen a bidet since she and Anton took their only trip to Europe, back in 1956.

She stood in the bathroom and stared at it, and decided that every time she felt a bit fuzzy about where she was and what she was doing, she'd go have a look at that bidet, which was bound to snap her back into reality.

The bidet wasn't the only funny thing in the place, either, not on your life.

"Dear Family," she wrote, in pencil, on the lined paper she'd brought from Marcia and Robbie's house. "Dear Family: I'm staying in a lovely little cottage just outside Sechelt. It's surrounded by trees that make nice soft swishing sounds. There are a lot of birds, too, starlings and sparrows, robins and bluejays."

She was sitting in the tiny kitchen, at a table that was round, made of wood, painted white, and had two sturdy matching chairs. The curtains were closed. Ramona had found a box of tacks in a drawer and covered the broken window with a piece of cardboard.

"It's very cozy here," she wrote. "Although I must admit it's an odd sort of place."

The cottage consisted of the kitchen, the bathroom, a living room, and a bedroom.

"They keep the television set in the bedroom," Ramona wrote to her brothers and sisters, "and they have a video machine, too, and a big collection of movies."

Almost the first thing she'd done after she moved in was put in a movie and turn it on. She watched for a minute or two, then sank onto the bed, her eyes wide and her mouth hanging open. She'd heard about movies like that, of course. Now she'd seen twenty-five of them.

"I am house-sitting here," she wrote, "and the owners have provided all the food and household supplies I need."

In the cupboards Ramona had found jars of macadamia nuts, tins of smoked oysters, boxes of English crackers, cans of peaches. In the fridge, several brands of imported beer, and many bottles of mineral water. In a cabinet in the living room, just about every kind of liquor and liqueur imaginable, plus a few bottles of wine.

Under the sink in the bathroom she had been relieved to discover three four-roll packages of toilet paper and several boxes of Kleenex.

"House-sitting is a very easy and pleasant job," Ramona told her family. "I wish I'd thought to do it years ago."

There was a film of dust over everything when she arrived. The cottage obviously hadn't been inhabited for months. Ramona had given it a thorough going-over, but she hadn't used the vacuum cleaner she found in the closet, because of the noise.

"It's very interesting, staying in other people's houses," she wrote. "What with the television, and the VCR, and all the books they've got here, I have a great deal to entertain me."

Every single book in the bookcase, which was in the living room, next to the Franklin stove, was about sex. One or two of them she recognized. She was amazed that some of them had been allowed to get printed.

"It's an extremely comfortable little house," she told her sisters and brothers. "I think that everything in it must have cost quite a lot of money."

She couldn't make a fire in the Franklin stove, of course. But luckily there was a space heater in the bedroom.

The brass bed was huge. When she got into it at night Ramona felt like an island adrift in a sea of bedding. She was certainly snug and warm, though, as she sat there sipping gin and watching television.

In the bedside table she'd found something she finally decided must be a—well, she wasn't sure exactly what it was called. But she thought she knew what it was for, by the shape of it.

"I'm writing so that you won't worry about me," she told her brothers and sisters. "Maybe Horace or Martha called one of you and told you I left the hospital. Well, this note is just to let you know that I'm just fine and enjoying myself a lot."

In the bedroom she'd also found ladies' underwear made of black lace, which was fine if you liked that sort of thing, but these pieces of underwear had great chunks missing from them, so that parts of the body could stick right out of them.

"I'll say goodbye now, and I'll drop you another line when I know where I'll be going next."

And most peculiar of all the peculiar things in this peculiar little house were the pieces of rope—soft rope, but rope just the same—that were tied onto the posts at the four corners of the bed.

Ramona had stood in the bedroom and looked at those pieces of rope and thought, and thought, frowning, chewing delicately on the inside of her lower lip. . . .

She considered untying them, getting rid of them.

But she decided to leave them there.

She folded her letter carefully and put it in the pocket of her dress, ready to be mailed just as soon as she came across an envelope and a stamp.

She stood up and opened the cupboard, looking for something to have for dinner, and then she heard a car.

Ramona hurried into the living room and pulled back the curtain just a smidgen. She watched as the sound of the engine got louder, and then she saw the Strachan woman's car pass slowly along the driveway, heading for the house, and it was thirty feet away and there were tree branches to peer between, but she was almost positive that in the seat next to the Strachan woman, who lived in that house all by herself, was a child.

CHAPTER

29

Alberg woke halfway through the night, feeling in the palms of his hands the shape of Zoe Strachan's ass.

He sat up in his bed and took his dream in his mind and looked at it.

In his dream they had been emerging from something, a room, a grove of trees—he wasn't sure, now, from what, exactly. He stood behind her. They faced, together, another person, maybe a group of people. They were emerging from privacy into the public world, but they carried, eloquently, their new intimacy with them.

Her hands were clasped in front of her. He stood behind her. His hands rested on her hips, a light embrace, casual, his hands bracketing her waist, lightly, and then he saw in the dream, and felt, his hands flex and trace the curve of her buttocks.

It was an intimate caress; and she was accepting of it. And the fact that he did not whisper to her, did not touch her neck, her temple, with his lips; the fact that he looked straight ahead at the person, or thing, or aspect, that they both observed, serenely, with almost all of their attention—this was the thing most sexually stirring to Alberg when he awoke.

He stroked her ass. She was letting him do it. And he knew that if he turned her around, her eyes would be bright, there would be a smile there for him; her mouth would open for his tongue. He knew it. He had experienced it, in his dream; and he knew, in his dream, that he would experience it again, the lustful appetite of Zoe Strachan.

"Jesus Christ," said Alberg in his bed, shaken.

CHAPTER
30

A potted yellow chrysanthemum sat on the counter of the second-floor nurses' station; it sported a dusty red bow, and a small card with "Thanks!" scrawled on it was attached to a metal spike that had been stuck into the soil.

"That thing's dying," said Cassandra to the nurse. It was lunchtime on Sunday.

Doris Moon looked at it hopefully. "Do you think so?"

"Is Mom still in her room?"

The nurse nodded. "Won't budge. Not for me, anyway."

Cassandra's mother was the only occupant of a four-bed ward. She lay propped up on two pillows, and the bed was slightly raised, too, so that she could look out the window at the lawn sweeping down to a gazebo that in summer was covered with climbing roses. The pathways that swirled lazily across the landscape were empty, glistening in the rain. In fine weather wheelchairs perambulated, nurses pushed IV stands, the walking wounded tottered from flower bed to flower bed.

"I hear they're going to tear that thing down," said Mrs. Mitchell, staring out the window at the gazebo, "and take the gardens out, and build an extended-care wing out there. Is that true?" She turned her head and saw that it was Cassandra standing there. Her face crumpled, and she began to cry.

Cassandra hurried to embrace her. "Mom. What's the matter?"

"Nobody told me you were coming," said her mother. "You didn't tell me you were coming now."

"I thought I'd see if they'd let me have lunch with you."

Her mother pulled away and fumbled at the box of tissues on the table beside her bed. "You should have asked me first," she said.

"Okay, Mom. May I have lunch with you?"

Her mother blew her nose into a handful of tissues.

"Maybe we could get them to give it to us in the solarium," said Cassandra.

Mrs. Mitchell made a sound of derision. "You call that a solarium?" She dropped the tissues into a metal wastebasket.

Cassandra sat in the chair next to the bed. Her mother wasn't wearing her reading glasses, and her face looked exposed and vulnerable. But her skin, though wrinkled, glowed, and her gray hair was soft and shining. "You're looking pretty good," said Cassandra. "When are they letting you out of here?"

"Alex is going to let me know today."

Cassandra reached out to stroke some hair away from her mother's cheek. Mrs. Mitchell pulled back, lifting a hand as if in self-defense. They looked at each other. Mrs. Mitchell lowered her hand.

"When I was little," said Cassandra, "you used to wash my hair in the sink, and then you'd rinse it, and then you'd fill the sink with cold water and add some vinegar and rinse it again in that."

"I remember."

"It got out all the leftover soap, you said. So that my hair could shine."

"I remember."

"But I always wondered—why did it have to be cold water?"

"It didn't have to be cold water." Mrs. Mitchell pushed the bedcovers back. "But it didn't have to be hot water, either." She swung her legs over the side of the bed. "And we were always counting our pennies. Come on, then. Hand me my robe. Let's go, if we're going."

The solarium had many windows, grand and wide. But all that could be seen through them was rain, heavy and tangible. It looked capable of entangling anyone trying to walk through it, of packaging him up in its thick wet strands. Through the skylights came a dense gray leakage of something purporting to be light.

In one corner sat an old man, thin and knobbly. He was wearing brown trousers, baggy at the knees, and a white shirt with the top button undone, both too big for him, and brown socks and a pair of worn leather slippers. Wide red plaid suspenders held up his pants. He sat with his knees apart, holding a cane, tilted forward somewhat, leaning on the cane, and his gaze was aimed at the floor. He didn't move when Cassandra and her mother entered the room.

In another corner a slim young woman wearing a blue terry-cloth robe over her hospital gown sat on a sofa with a man Cassandra thought was probably her husband. He was holding her hands and talking to her quietly. She listened intently; every so often she nodded.

There was a console television set near the elderly man. It

was tuned to a gardening program from Victoria, but the sound was off.

Mrs. Mitchell moved away from Cassandra and headed for a large schleffera that sat in a plastic pot near the windows. She reached down and stuck a finger in the soil. "Look at this," she said, as Cassandra approached. She rubbed some of the soil between her fingers. "Completely dried out." She looked around the room for support, but nobody was paying attention. "I didn't bring my glasses," she said, peering at the leaves of the plant. "Can you see any dust?"

"Oh, yes," said Cassandra.

"And they call it a damned solarium," said Mrs. Mitchell violently. "No damn sun, one plant, nobody looks after it." She shook her head. Her eyes glittered with tears.

"Who's for lunch?" said a voice from the doorway.

"We are," said Cassandra gratefully. "That is, my mother is."

"I've got coffee and sandwiches for the visitors," said the nurse, wheeling in a cart. "Can't let you go home hungry."

The elderly man raised his head. "When are they coming for me, then?"

"It's the doctor that's coming, Mr. Simpson," said the nurse. "He'll be along soon." She pulled a TV tray from a stack leaning against the wall and set it up in front of him. "Meanwhile you might as well have your lunch."

"I can't stand this," Mrs. Mitchell hissed in Cassandra's ear. "I want to go back to my room."

"Let's eat first, Mom," Cassandra whispered. "She's gone to all the trouble of bringing it here. Have lunch, then I'll take you back to your room." She nudged her mother gently down onto the sofa and sat next to her.

Mr. Simpson regarded the food being arrayed before him

with an expression of amazement, as though he couldn't imagine what its purpose might be.

"There you are," said the nurse. "Dig in."

"I'll wait for my brother," said Mr. Simpson. "I told him to meet me here."

Mrs. Mitchell stood up. "I'm going back to my room," she said, and Cassandra hurried to follow her. "You can't get a moment's peace in this place," said Mrs. Mitchell angrily, "unless you keep to your own room, your own bed." She hurried along the hall, past the nurses' station and into her room.

"There you are!" Alex Gillingham beamed. "I thought you'd escaped!" He leaned toward them. "Did you hear about Ramona?"

Helen Mitchell looked at him and began to cry again.

"Mom," said Cassandra, helpless and exasperated.

Dr. Gillingham put his arms around Cassandra's mother. "There, there," he said, giving Cassandra a reassuring nod. "I'm sending you home tomorrow, Helen. It's too damn depressing around here."

Cassandra felt suddenly exhausted. She slumped into the chair.

Mrs. Mitchell pressed her lips together, wrapped her robe tightly around her, and clambered back into bed.

"All you need now is rest," said the doctor. "And you don't get a hell of a lot of that in a hospital."

"What on earth's wrong with you now?" said Helen Mitchell accusingly. "You're limping."

"Took a spill on a climb last weekend," said Gillingham proudly. "Nothing serious."

"I saw Marjorie the other day," said Mrs. Mitchell. "Crank

this bed up a bit more, will you, Cassandra? She's looking well. Very well, as a matter of fact."

"That's good," said Gillingham indulgently. "I'm glad to hear it. I remain very fond of Marjorie."

"Dyed her hair."

He looked at her in astonishment. "Who, Marjorie?"

"Blond."

"Marjorie?"

"Suits her very well."

"Blond?"

"She's a pleasant woman, Marjorie. I always liked her."

"How's that, Mom?" said Cassandra. "High enough?"

"Just fine, thank you, Cassandra."

"I can't imagine Marjorie with blond hair," said Gillingham, frowning. "I keep seeing Jean Harlow in my head."

"She looks as she always looked," said Mrs. Mitchell. "Except that her hair is blond. And she's lost about thirty pounds."

"You don't say."

"She's got a boyfriend, too, or so I hear."

"Good Christ." Gillingham limped back toward the door. "That's enough. Don't tell me any more."

"You're not going to find another woman the likes of Marjorie up on top of some mountain, you know, Alex."

"I don't think that's what he goes up there looking for, Mom," said Cassandra. She took a furtive peek at her watch.

"It's no way for a man your age to be spending his spare time. All you're going to do is find a way to maim yourself for life," said Mrs. Mitchell with relish. "Or kill yourself entirely."

"It can be more dangerous indoors than out, Helen," said Gillingham. He leaned casually against the doorframe. "You know I do some work for the Mounties? Well, I was out on a call the other day. A chap fell down some basement stairs. Deader than a doornail."

Helen Mitchell looked shocked. "Who? I haven't heard a word about it. Who was it?"

"You know that Strachan woman? Her brother. Visiting her from West Vancouver." He made a plunging motion with one hand. "Down the stairs, right onto his head."

"The poor woman," said Mrs. Mitchell sympathetically. "How awful for her."

"Actually," said Gillingham, "it didn't seem to bother her a whit. Not one whit. Decidedly unsisterlike she is, that one." He glanced at Cassandra. "I think Karl noticed it, too," he said, and Cassandra's heart gave a gentle lurch.

Then they were both looking at her, her mother from the bed, Alex Gillingham from the doorway. Cassandra, sitting, felt overweight and frumpy. She was afraid she was going to blush.

"I forgot to tell you, Mom," she blurted. "Karl said to say hello."

"Karl who?" said her mother coldly.

"Karl Alberg, Helen," said Gillingham, grinning.

"Oh yes," said Mrs. Mitchell vaguely. "The policeman."

"Now, I don't want you to be on your own just yet," said the doctor. "Can you stay with Cassandra for a few days? Say, 'til the end of the week?"

"Oh I'm sure that won't be convenient, Alex," said Mrs. Mitchell. "My daughter leads a very busy life." She looked appraisingly at Cassandra. "Too busy for her own good. I worry about you, Cassandra, really I do. Here you've been back from England for—what, a week? Two weeks? And already you're off somewhere else. She's going to Victoria," she said wearily to Gillingham, "for a few days. Oh I can't keep up with her, this one."

Cassandra sighed, picked up her shoulder bag, and stood up. Shit, she thought.

CHAPTER

31

Alberg, tying his tie in his Calgary motel on Monday morning, studied his receding hairline with dismay. Blond hair was good, at least it didn't show the gray, but at this rate he soon wouldn't have hair of any color at all up there.

In July he would be fifty. His stomach did a kind of flip whenever he thought about that.

Still, he knew that a lot of women preferred men who'd reached a certain level of maturity.

He had to lose some weight. Fifteen pounds anyway. Maybe twenty. No muscle there anymore, he thought, distractedly hitting himself in the diaphragm—he'd always prided himself on his ability to take a blow to the stomach. He was pure fat now, pure damn fat. Of course that wasn't true, he thought, staring into the mirror. There *was* muscle there. Of course there was.

A guy like Sanducci, girlfriends strewn all over the

peninsula . . . that was all well and good, fine, but what did a guy like that have to offer a real woman, an adult female, someone seductive, yes, and attractive, sure—but someone who was discriminating, as well.

He squirted something called European Styling Foam into his hand and rubbed it on his hair and combed it and patted it until it decided to stay down. Now he had a wet spot on the top of his head. It'll dry, he told himself, long before I get there. He realized that he wasn't looking forward much to the afternoon, and this dismayed him.

He had enjoyed spending the previous day with his daughters. But it had made him sad, too, and resentful. Who the hell knew when he'd see them again?

Why couldn't all of them have ended up in Central Canada, near his parents, instead of way the hell and gone out here in the West, near Maura's? It wasn't fair to Diana and Janey not to have the steadying influence of their other grandparents, who possessed a bit of damn dignity, who saw things clearly, as they really were, not as they damn wanted to see them. His kids had grown up thinking of themselves as Westerners, just because they were born here, and this despite the fact that they had a whole damn clutch of relatives in Ontario, despite the fact that their own damn father had been born out there.

He washed his hands and dried them and put on his jacket.

On a day like this everybody should be there, he thought. All four of their grandparents should be here, not just half of them. But Alberg's father wasn't well, and his mother wouldn't travel without her husband.

Alberg placed another call to Sechelt.

"She hasn't turned up yet," said Sokolowski. "We've been checking the house. No sign of her."

"Damn," said Alberg. "We better do another search of the

area, Sid. Maybe she went for a walk, fell down, broke her hip or some damn thing."

"Yeah. I'll get on it."

"Any word from Gillingham?"

"No. Why?"

"He's got a bee in his bonnet over this Strachan thing."

"What do you mean?"

"Oh, hell, nothing. There's a wound, there's a bruise or some damn thing; Gillingham's got it into his head maybe it wasn't an accident."

"Oh, yeah?" Sokolowski hesitated, then said, "Well, I don't like the guy, you know that, Staff. But I gotta admit, he's good."

"He's good, yeah. But he's full of shit on this one."

"You'll be back this afternoon, right?"

"It'll be evening by the time I get to Sechelt."

"If Gillingham gets the report over here today I'll make sure it's on your desk."

"Okay. Thanks, Sid."

Alberg buttoned his jacket, looked at himself in the mirror, unbuttoned it, turned left and right, put his hands casually in his pockets, took them out, buttoned the jacket and straightened up, studied himself some more. Shit on it, he said, finally, and undid the buttons. He patted his pockets, checking for his wallet, and collected car keys and room key from the top of the dresser.

Then he took two small gift-wrapped boxes from the desk and put them carefully in one of his jacket pockets.

He was ready to go.

Hundreds and hundreds of students were graduating that day from the University of Calgary. Hundreds and hundreds of cars, it seemed to Alberg, were trying to find places to park there. Maura and her parents had decided to travel by cab and had offered to pick up Alberg on their way, but he had declined. Now he wished he hadn't.

It was still cold and gray—though at least, thank God, it wasn't snowing—and he hoped his daughters would be warm enough in their graduation robes as they walked in the procession to the gymnasium.

Somehow in the crowd Maura spotted him and waved and shouted until he saw her. He had hoped to sneak in unobserved and bury himself among the hordes, but when he saw her he was glad. She led him to a seat somewhere near the rafters of the building, shouting, "We should have gotten here a good hour ago. I had no idea people would come so early."

When the ceremonies finally got under way Alberg realized that the place was an acoustic disaster. It was impossible to hear anything being said on the stage below. Appreciative laughter washed upward from time to time, apparently in response to witticisms emitted by the various honorary-degree recipients, the president of the university, and God only knew who else.

Alberg had missed his own graduation, having opted to pay a hasty visit to his parents, instead, before reporting to the RCMP training center in Regina. So he had imagined being overcome at the graduation of his daughters; he had expected to have to struggle not to let tears spring to his eyes; he had thought he might have to put an arm around Maura, comforting her as she wept. Now he was chagrined because Maura was calm and dry-eyed and he himself didn't feel a single damn thing except irritation because he couldn't hear the names as they were called out.

His mind wandered. To Cassandra. To Benjamin Strachan.

To Zoe. He wondered what she did for a living. Maybe Isabella was right. Maybe she was a model.

When the ceremonies were over, Maura and her parents went ahead by cab to the restaurant where they were all to have lunch and present Janey and Diana with their graduation gifts. Alberg said he would wait for his daughters to get rid of their gowns, and take them to the restaurant in his rented car.

He stationed himself at the foot of the steps that led down from the gym. People were still spilling out of the building, and all around him graduating students were being embraced, wept over, smiled upon, and photographed. Alberg had forgotten to bring his own little point-and-shoot.

He waited impatiently, shivering in his too-light jacket, wondering what the hell could be keeping them; after all, he had a plane to catch. He glanced at his watch, looked up again—and there they were, just a few feet away from him, standing on the steps and scanning the faces in the crowd below; they had stopped moving down the stairs, and people had to go around them, but nobody seemed to mind.

Janey stood on the step behind Diana, the fingers of her right hand resting lightly on Diana's shoulder. They wore black robes and mortarboards, and their faces were unexpectedly grave. They were looking for him among the throngs of parents; he was astonished at how beautiful they were.

He knew that he was living one of those moments that freeze themselves forever in memory; how much better this is, he thought, than a photograph.

When they saw him their faces became so radiant that he held out his arms, helpless, and they ran down the rest of the steps and he hugged them and offered them summer jobs in Sechelt.

* * *

Later, feeling melancholy, he drove his rented car to the airport. He was standing in the Air Canada check-in line when he felt a hand on his arm.

"Maura," he said, delighted.

"I decided I wanted to see you off," she said. She was wearing a long gray coat with a red scarf around her neck, black boots, and a black handbag slung over her shoulder. "The kids wanted to come, too. But I wouldn't let them."

Alberg reached the counter and handed over his ticket. He checked his bag, even though it was small enough to fit under the seat, and got a boarding pass.

"Maybe there's time for coffee," he said, taking Maura by the arm. They went upstairs to the cafeteria.

"So you're going to give your daughters jobs this summer," said Maura once they were seated.

"Yeah," he said, beaming. "I haven't a damn clue what they'll be. But I'll think of something."

Maura had dark eyes and a dark complexion. She wore her hair short and straight, and she was tall and elegantly thin. Alberg gazed at her fondly. "They're good kids, aren't they," he said.

"Yes, Karl. They are."

Janey, who looked like her mother, had travelled for a year after graduating from high school. That was a year Alberg would never forget. He was constantly on the phone to Maura, wanting to know where Janey was, and what she was doing; what trouble she'd gotten herself into. She didn't get into any trouble at all. At least, none that Alberg had been made aware of.

Diana, who resembled Alberg's Aunt Dorothea on his father's side, was two years younger than her sister. She had skipped a year in elementary school, and she went straight from high school to university. Thus it was that the two of them had gone through university together.

"They loved your gifts," said Maura. He had given them silver jewelry, a locket for Janey and a bracelet for Diana, created by a West Coast Indian artist.

"Oh, yeah? Do you think so?" But he already knew, from their reactions, that he had pleased them.

"What are they going to do between now and the summer?" he asked their mother.

"They're coming back with me. Diana says she'll be my housekeeper. Janey's going to help in the shop for a few weeks." Maura owned a women's clothing store in Kamloops, a small city in the interior of British Columbia. "Then I think she's going to go to California with a friend."

"What?" said Alberg. "What friend? Why haven't I heard about this?"

"You're hearing about it right now. And I'm sure Janey will be happy to tell you anything I've left out."

"What kind of a friend?"

"You mean, is it a boyfriend? No."

"Damn good thing, too," said Alberg, relaxing slightly.

"How are you doing, Karl?"

He opened his mouth to say a few hearty things, reassuring but impersonal, but he found that he couldn't.

Maura's face reflected the serenity that had always haunted him. It was her private possession, precious and unshareable: an inner strength, a self-assurance that he deeply envied. He often thought that their marriage had been sacrificed to Maura's serenity; that when it came to the crunch, her tranquillity was more important to Maura than he had been.

He saw her regarding him, quite openly, with great affection, and he sighed and said, "Well. Let's see. I like the job, of course. I like Sechelt. And I like the people there. I've got a couple of cats. I'm kind of lonely," he said bravely, "from time to time."

"I thought you were seeing someone," said Maura. "A librarian. Or is that over with?"

Alberg, flustered, said, "Over—no, it's not over; it—" Upon a screen somewhere in his mind flashed Zoe Strachan's face, pensive and luminous. He opened his mouth to say something that would replace her image with Cassandra's; he just needed a minute, only a minute, to find the right words. . . .

"Good," said his ex-wife warmly. "By the way, Karl. I want you to know . . . I'm getting married again."

He gawked at her. His hand gave a convulsive jerk, striking his cup, which overturned and spilled black coffee all over the tabletop. He sprang to his feet, to avoid getting it on his good pants. "Shit." He looked at Maura in despair. "Oh, good," he said.

She pushed her chair away from the table and stood up.

"That's grand, Maura."

She brushed coffee from the front of her gray coat and put her arms around him, firmly.

"Oh, I'm happy for you."

"I know you are, Karl. I know you are."

CHAPTER
32

In the plane Alberg mulled and fretted and worried; who was this son of a bitch she was going to marry? Marry! He shuddered. How had this come about?

While driving from the Vancouver airport to Gibsons he regretted, lamented, and grieved. He didn't even get out of his car on the ferry; he was too weak with self-pity. He refused to remember the guy's name. Maura had said he was an accountant. Also divorced. With no children of his own. Christ, thought Alberg. The accountant might have had children of his own. Maura might have become somebody's stepmother. Janey and Diana might have acquired stepbrothers, and stepsisters. Alberg was aghast.

All night long, it seemed, he brooded, he languished, he mourned. He began seeing Maura in his mind with a shadow at her shoulder. At first the shadow was tall, broad, ominous. Pitilessly, Alberg cut him down to size. Still he remained there, no longer ominous but stubborn as hell, right at Maura's shoulder; Alberg could almost hear him panting and slavering back there, refusing to leave her, clinging to her neck. Jesus. Then he became indignant. When Tuesday dawned he was sitting up in bed, mad as hell, waiting until it was no longer too early to phone Calgary. What the hell was she up to, getting married? What did his kids think about this, he'd like to know.

When it was late enough to phone Calgary he decided to phone Cassandra instead. He needed sympathy. Kindness. Tenderness. Of course in order to get these things he'd have to tell her he needed them; she wasn't a mind reader, after all. And then she'd want to know why he needed them. He didn't know how she'd react when he told her he was suffering because his ex-wife was getting married again.

In the end it was all academic, because Cassandra's mother was out of the hospital and staying with her daughter. He could hear in Cassandra's voice that her teeth were clenched, figuratively at least, probably literally as well. Alberg heaved a sigh and suggested lunch, but of course she had to go home at noon to make lunch for her mother. They were at cross-purposes, Alberg with his preoccupation and Cassandra with hers, and when he hung up he felt sad and achy.

At the detachment, things weren't much better. Isabella informed him that Sid Sokolowski's wife's cousin, whose name was Ludmilla, wanted to apply for the job as his cleaning woman. Alberg didn't want to hire a relative of Sid Sokolowski's as his cleaning woman. But she was there, in person, waiting, so of course he had to see her. She was a young, strong, brawny, intelligent woman with big red hands and a lot of thick yellow hair. He looked at her and quailed inside. He gave her a weak smile, asked a few questions, heard her out, and sent her courteously on her way. God only knew what possible reason he could give Sid for not hiring her, but he wasn't going to hire her, and that was that. I don't think I'll hire anybody, he decided, and said it aloud to himself, in his office, looking at the phone, imagining the conversation he was about to have with Janey and Diana.

For he had to call them. He was pretty sure they already knew about Maura and the accountant, and he had to let them know that he was okay, that he was happy for her and all that shit. Then maybe he'd get some sympathy from them. He sure as hell needed to get some from somebody.

And then the phone rang, and it was Gillingham.

"All right, all right. I'm releasing the Strachan fellow for burial," said the doctor.

"Good," said Alberg. "It's about time."

"That woman doesn't have a phone, for Christ's sake. I've got better things to do than trundle all over town delivering corpses. How about if you dispatch one of your guys over to her house. Tell her she can have him picked up anytime."

"I'm glad you changed your mind," said Alberg.

"I haven't damn changed my mind. I do not like that wound on his head. I do not like the bruise in his gut. I do not like his damn sister, who as much as said he was sloshed to the gills, and he wasn't." He sighed. "But the head wound didn't kill him. Falling down the stairs killed him."

"And he could have—"

"Yeah yeah yeah. You're right. He could have gotten the smack on the head when he fell. So I owe you an apology. I guess I've been wasting my time."

"It happens to all of us," said Alberg.

He hung up the phone and stretched. He linked his hands behind his head and surveyed the ceiling. After a while, "I'll do it myself," he muttered. "I could do with a break."

He told Isabella where he was going, and headed off to see Zoe Strachan.

A few minutes later he pulled up in front of her house, walked up to the heavy double doors, and rang the bell. He heard it echo faintly through the house. He rubbed his feet on the mat and lifted first one shoe, then the other, to polish the tops of them on his pantlegs.

It had begun to rain, very lightly; Alberg heard raindrops landing among the boughs of the arbutus trees, and splatting on the overhang above the door, and on the driveway. But they were falling slowly, dreamily. A gust of wind came up and set the arbutus chattering. He rang the doorbell again. Apparently she wasn't home.

He pressed his ear to the door and heard nothing from within the house. He rang the bell again, just to make some sound happen in there.

Alberg shoved his hands in his pockets and looked around at Zoe Strachan's property. After a minute he decided to circle the house.

There were two windows in the side wall that faced southeast, toward the easternmost of the Trail Islands and beyond to Mission Point. Alberg glanced through them as he plodded past upon grass slippery with rain that was quickening, and thickening. When he turned the corner the grass ended and the patio began, chunks of flat, rough stone placed side by side and glued together with cement. At the back of the patio was a jumble of enormous boulders. Behind them Alberg saw the gunmetal sea and the Trail Islands.

The rain was falling hard now, rippling the ocean, and Alberg crossed the patio quickly with his shoulders hunched, pulling up the collar of his jacket. He couldn't see much anyway, even though this side of the house was almost all glass, because venetian blinds shuttered out his curious glances; he knew without trying them that the French doors would be locked, and why would he try them anyway? He had no right to be poking around Zoe Strachan's house.

Alberg waited for a minute in the shelter of the overhang, before turning to head back to his car.

Then, for no good reason, he stopped, and stepped around behind the house again. With the wind pushing at his back and the rain plastering his hair to his head, he saw the blind covering the nearer set of French doors move slightly. The space between two of the narrow horizontal slats widened, widened; and Alberg thought he saw a face. The blind returned slowly to its original position. Alberg waited, quizzical, disbelieving; and there it was again—a pale face, small and young, with enormous eyes. Definitely not Zoe Strachan's face. Alberg didn't move, but he smiled, and lifted his hand, slowly, and gave the small face a salute; he tried to put into his smile, into the salute, whatever there was in him that was warm and unthreatening. The face continued to look out at him; then Alberg heard a car approaching over the gravel driveway, and the blind dropped, the face disappeared.

C H A P T E R

33

Zoe Strachan signaled and turned across the highway into her driveway, and made her way slowly along the promontory, thinking about the boy, wondering if he had remained in the house, as she'd instructed him.

But where could he go, for heaven's sake?

He might have taken it into his head to hitchhike to the ferry. Except that he had no money for the ferry.

Maybe he'd hitchhiked into Sechelt, then, to telephone a friend. He probably did have one or two friends.

These things had been going through her mind as she shopped, and now she was impatient to get inside and make sure that he was in fact still there.

She saw a white car parked near her front door, and the staff sergeant standing on her doorstep.

She opened the garage door with the automatic gadget and drove inside. She was out of the car, carrying her handbag and her shopping, before the door had descended.

"What do you want?" she said. "What are you doing here?"

"Could we go inside?" Alberg hunched his shoulders.

He was a big man, which she liked, but he was a little flabby around the waist; he didn't drive a police car, he didn't wear a uniform—he wasn't Zoe's idea of a policeman at all. He was a dissembler, that's what he was. People ought to be what they appeared to be, not to go around trying to look like something else.

"I'd like to get out of the rain," he said.

"You can get out of the rain by climbing into your car and driving away."

Alberg smiled at her. She watched the raindrops tumble down his face and saw that he wanted to touch her.

"I have business with you, Miss Strachan," he said. "Could we please go inside?"

There seem to be an awful lot of people cluttering up my life these days, Zoe thought irritably.

She walked through the rain to the door and unlocked it. "Come in, then," she said.

Alberg followed her across the threshold and into the small tiled entryway, empty except for an umbrella stand in the corner by the door and a library table against one wall.

Zoe Strachan set down her purse and her plastic shopping bag on the library table, opened a closet door, and hung up her raincoat. As she turned back to face him she ran her hands over her hips, smoothing her black skirt, smoothing it again. It wasn't a flirtatious gesture; he thought she wasn't even aware of it; she looked too preoccupied. Alberg heard the whisper of her hands against the fabric of the skirt and saw again the strange blankness in her eyes and wondered if she spoke aloud while making love.

He waited for her to call out to the child, but she didn't.

"What business do you have with me?" she said, closing the closet door. She tugged at the cuffs of her sweater, an emerald-green pullover, until they covered her wrists. "I presume it's about my brother."

Her eyes were blue but they looked green today, because of the sweater. They were very beautiful eyes. Maybe they weren't empty after all, he thought. Maybe they only seemed empty because she wasn't interested in him. He knew from the way she looked at him that she wasn't interested in him.

"Who's the child?" he said, more roughly than he had intended.

Zoe Strachan blinked. "What child?" She said it automatically.

"The one I saw staring at me from between the slats of the venetian blinds."

She gazed at him for a moment. He could see that she was interested now, all right. He was incongruously pleased with himself, as if he'd conjured up the boy who'd peeked at him from behind the blinds, created him from nothing, then presented him to Zoe Strachan as a surprise. His face felt open and eager; he tried to close it off from her.

"Apparently," said Zoe Strachan slowly, "he's Benjamin's son."

"I thought you said your brother had no family. Except you."

She nodded, studying him. "I know what I said." She picked up her purse and the plastic bag and walked slowly down the hall. He watched her body move under the black skirt and heard again the swish of silk, or nylon, or whatever the hell they used in the making of stockings. When she reached the kitchen she turned and said, "Sit down in here. I'll be back in a minute. I have to take him these clothes."

Alberg watched from the kitchen doorway as she went into the living room, then out again. She opened a door at the end of the hall and disappeared for a moment to put away her purse. She opened the next door. "There you are," she said, and went inside. Alberg heard murmurings but no words. She emerged almost immediately, without the shopping bag, and joined Alberg in the kitchen. "I'm going to make coffee," she said. "Will you have some?"

"Thank you. Yes."

"Sit down," said Zoe.

Alberg sat down at the table. "What's his name? I'd like to meet him," he said.

She turned from the cupboard, the coffee canister in her hand. "You would?" she said, and looked astonished.

"Sure," said Alberg. "I like kids."

"Really," said Zoe. She shook her head and began measuring coffee into the pot.

"Why do you think your brother never told you about him?"

"Benjamin was a curious person," she said vaguely. "It was difficult to know why he did anything."

"How did you find out about him? Your nephew."

She hesitated. "I went to the house," she said, leaning against the counter. She crossed her arms. "I thought I'd better get some of Benjamin's clothes. To bury him in."

"Ah," said Alberg. He was gazing intently into her face, trying not to look at her breasts.

"I have his keys," she added.

"Oh, yes," said Alberg. "That's right."

"It was a very good thing that I went, too," she said, nodding. "Because there he was. The boy. All by himself. Heaven knows what would have become of him."

"How old is he?"

She looked thoughtful. "Ten, I think he said."

"Then he goes to school."

"I'm sure he does."

"He has friends; teachers. He would have called someone."

"Oh, yes. I see what you mean. I suppose he would have." She poured water into the coffeepot and turned it on. He wished she'd sit down at the table with him.

"But it's much better that a relative happened along," said Alberg.

She gave him a glance that was almost amused. Then she got two cups and saucers from a cupboard and put them on the table. As she leaned across him he could smell her perfume.

"He's adopted," said Zoe. "So I'm not actually his relative."

"She's my dad's relative," said a voice, and Alberg turned to see a child in the doorway.

He was small and wiry, with brown hair and large brown eyes. He looked pale and tired.

Alberg smiled at him. "I hope I didn't scare you," he said. "When I was looking at the house, and you were looking out."

The boy's eyes flickered to Zoe, and back to Alberg. "No," he said.

"I told you to stay in your room," said Zoe pleasantly.

The boy looked at her, and then at Alberg. "My name's Kenny. Kenneth. I'm nine. I'll be ten in seven weeks."

"So you're—let me work this out—you're in grade four, right?"

"Right." The boy eased into the room, his back pressed against the wall. "Who're you?"

"My name is Karl. I'm a policeman. A Mountie," he added, just in case the kid was still young enough to be favorably impressed.

"I think you should go back to your room," said Zoe.

"I will," said Kenny, looking at Alberg. "My dad died," he said.

Alberg nodded. "I know. I'm very sorry."

"He fell down some stairs."

"I know. You must miss him a lot."

"Where?" said Kenny.

Alberg leaned forward slightly. "Pardon?"

"What stairs?"

Alberg looked at Zoe.

"I don't think we should talk about it," she said to the child. "I want you to go back to your room now. You can watch television." As she approached him, Alberg saw him shrink back. "Come," she said. She reached out to touch him, or take his hand, but Kenny pulled quickly away—and Zoe made a sudden, savage grab at the boy's shoulder.

"Hey," said Alberg, his hand outstretched in protest. He scraped back his chair, intending to stand up.

But just as suddenly as she had taken hold of the boy she let him go, and straightened. Kenny ducked under her arm and skittered off toward his room.

Zoe turned to Alberg. "Excuse me," she said graciously. Alberg watched, attentive, as she followed the boy down the hall.

"What are you going to do with him?" he said when she returned.

"I'm going to keep him for a while," said Zoe.

She smiled at him, and Alberg felt his mouth go dry. She was thinking about him. He knew there was nothing at all on her mind except him. It was like staring into a searchlight.

"He has grandparents," Zoe went on. "His mother's parents. He'll go to live with them, I expect. After the funeral."

He nodded, smiling a little, looking into her eyes. He wondered if she could see inside his mind.

"Perhaps you can tell me, Staff Sergeant—when is that doctor going to release the body?"

He felt his smile become fixed and heard himself say, "Soon. I'm sure it'll be soon." She looked startled, and he realized that he'd stood up. He turned and headed quickly for the front door.

"Aren't you going to have coffee?" she said, following him.

"I'll check back with Dr. Gillingham right away," he said over his shoulder, "and find out when you can claim the body."

"But I thought—why did you come here, then?" she said, annoyed.

On her front step he peered worriedly up into the sky. "Still raining. Doesn't look like it's about to quit, either." He pulled up the collar of his jacket. "I'll be back soon," he said to her.

He trotted off into the rain, and Zoe, baffled, watched him go. Perhaps he'll get pneumonia, she thought crossly, and cough himself to death.

CHAPTER
34

Cassandra sat in her living room watching television, acutely mindful of her mother's supine presence on the white leather sofa. The sound of Mrs. Mitchell's chortling response to Bill Cosby rasped in Cassandra's ears. The sight of her mother pursing her lips to drink tea caused Cassandra to blink rapidly, as though it were a mote in her eye. The fragrance of Helen Mitchell's lavender bath salts, bath powder, and body cream created an unpleasant tickling at the back of Cassandra's nose.

When "The Cosby Show" was over, Mrs. Mitchell switched over to "Matlock." "I've always liked Andy Griffith," she said approvingly.

"How come you never got married again?" said Cassandra abruptly.

"You know why," said her mother comfortably. "I never met a man who could hold a candle to your father."

Cassandra's father had died when she was eight. When she thought of him, which wasn't often, she recalled a distant benevolence that seemed always to have been attired in a gray suit. He'd died in 1951, and Cassandra's mother had embraced widowhood as if she'd been born to it.

"I know, Mom," said Cassandra. "But you must have met some who would have made a pretty decent second choice."

"I had children to bring up," said Mrs. Mitchell. "You and Graham. You were my first responsibility."

Cassandra's brother, Graham, was seven years older than she. His memories of their father were sharp and clear and legion. Sometimes when the three of them got together and started reminiscing, Cassandra tried to chime in with some memories of her own. But the other two always corrected her, and added things, and soon whatever it was she'd thought she remembered was unrecognizable. Defunct.

Cassandra stood up. "I'm going to bed," she said. "Can I get you anything first?"

"It's not even nine o'clock," said her mother. "Do you always go to bed so early?"

"No," said Cassandra. "I'm just tired today, that's all. Can I get you something?"

"Well, it's a bit early, but I suppose I could have my hot milk now, if it's not too much trouble."

Cassandra slept badly that night.

When she awoke Tuesday morning she heard her mother talking to someone. She dressed hurriedly and found Mrs. Mitchell in the kitchen, sitting at the table talking on the phone to Graham.

Cassandra made her bed, washed, combed her hair, and put on some makeup. Her mother was still talking. She sounded cheerful and happy. When Cassandra went back to the kitchen to start making breakfast, her mother said, "Here, dear, say hello to your brother," and held out the phone.

"I don't want to say hello to my brother," said Cassandra, opening a cupboard.

"I'd better go now, Graham," said Mrs. Mitchell. When she'd hung up she said, "I always call him early in the morning. The rates are cheaper before eight."

Cassandra, making coffee, didn't reply.

"Make sure you let me know, when the bill comes, how much I owe you for long-distance calls," said her mother.

The phone rang, and it was Karl. He sounded plaintive and depressed. He invited her out to lunch; Cassandra said no, she'd have to make lunch for her mother.

She got orange juice out of the fridge and poured herself a glass.

"None for me, dear," said her mother. "It's too acidic for my stomach. I'll just have some milk and cereal. What's more," she said, standing up, slowly, "I think I can get it for myself this morning."

"Sit down," said Cassandra. "I'll get it."

"No, no," said Mrs. Mitchell, shuffling across the room toward the pantry. "I'm going to do it."

"Mother. If you're well enough to fix your own breakfast, you're probably well enough to go home. Are you well enough to go home?"

Tears quivered in Mrs. Mitchell's eyes, but Cassandra could tell she was becoming angry. "Why are you being unkind?" said her mother.

Cassandra sat down at the table. "I don't know. I'm sorry."

Her mother was too short to reach the cereal, which was on the top shelf, so Cassandra got it for her. She sat down again and watched as Mrs. Mitchell carefully poured cereal into a bowl, and added milk, and got a spoon from the silverware drawer.

Her mother had to pass behind Cassandra in order to return to her place at the table, and as she did so, Cassandra automatically flinched.

When he left Zoe Strachan, Alberg went to Cassandra's house; it was Tuesday, and he knew the library didn't open until one o'clock on Tuesdays, so he was pretty sure she'd be home. He drove past the hospital, up the hill, onto the gravel access road that paralleled the highway. Cassandra's garage door was open, and her fourteen-year-old Hornet was parked inside.

He went up the walk and was surprised to hear an argument going on inside. He knocked on the door. After a minute he heard angry whispering, and a door slamming, and quick footsteps approaching. The door opened. Cassandra stood there, looking feverish.

"Do you know," said Alberg solemnly, "that a domestic dispute is the thing us police dread most?"

Cassandra's face flushed crimson. "Did somebody call you?" she said, appalled.

Alberg laughed. "No. I was just passing by." He glanced over her shoulder into the house, but he couldn't see Mrs. Mitchell. "Is everything okay?"

"Everything is fine," said Cassandra. "What do you want?" He watched affectionately as she brushed some stray strands of hair from her forehead. He loved the way it got curlier when it got damp.

"Oh," he said softly, "I just needed to get my lust in perspective." Her skin looked very warm; there was a thin blaze of sweat on her face.

"What are you talking about?" she said impatiently.

"Actually, I thought I'd wait while you make lunch for your mom, and then take you to Earl's. So we can plan our trip."

"Trip? What trip?"

"What do you mean, 'what trip'?" he said indignantly. "We're going to Victoria. This weekend."

She shook her head wearily. "I can't go away this weekend, Karl."

"You mean . . . your mother?" He lowered his voice. "But I thought you said there wasn't anything wrong with her."

"Talk to your friend Gillingham," she snapped. "It was his idea."

"Shit."

"Thirteen years this has been going on. For thirteen years I've lived in this godforsaken town, watching over my damn mother, who might or might not have a damn heart condition."

"Cassandra. Calm down."

"Oh calm down yourself for God's sake. Why are you standing there, anyway? Go away. Go find somebody else to go to Victoria with." She slammed the door.

CHAPTER
35

When Alberg got to the detachment a few minutes later, Sandy McAllister, the mailman, was there talking to Isabella, and Sid Sokolowski was helping himself over at the coffee machine.

"Look at that rain," said Isabella. "I think we need a few flowers in here, to brighten the place up."

"Forget it," said Alberg.

"I'll get some tomorrow," said Isabella. "Maybe a pot of hyacinths. Wait a minute before you disappear down your hallway there. You've got another chance to see Bernie Peters. She can squeeze you in tomorrow afternoon."

"I've changed my mind, Isabella," said Alberg, with a furtive glance at the reproachful back of Sid Sokolowski, whose wife's cousin Ludmilla he had turned down for the job. "I'm not going to hire anybody after all." He scurried into his office and shut the door before she could come after him.

Then he called Gillingham. "I need to talk to you," he said, and they arranged to meet at Earl's for lunch.

* * *

Gillingham ordered a spinach salad and some soda water. Alberg asked for a hamburger platter and coffee.

"I went out to see Zoe Strachan," Alberg told the doctor. "I didn't tell her she can have the body."

Gillingham stared at him. "You're kidding."

"I changed my mind," said Alberg defensively.

Gillingham held up his hand. "Wait. Let me guess. There's another dead guy in her basement."

"No. But there's a kid in her spare room."

"What kind of a kid?"

"Small. Male. In seven weeks he'll be ten years old."

Earl, the Chinese owner of the café, delivered Alberg's coffee in a large mug.

"Jesus, Earl," said the doctor, "what are you trying to do, kill him?"

"He likes his coffee," said Earl, setting down Gillingham's soda water. "What can I do? If I don't supply him, somebody else will."

"It's her brother's kid," said Alberg, when Earl had retreated.

"The dead guy? I thought you told me he didn't have any kids."

"Yeah. She says she didn't know about him. He's adopted. Kenny, his name is."

Gillingham sat back and watched approvingly as Earl put down a large bowl of spinach salad, dressing on the side. "I'm not going to say a word about that crap you're feeding to my overweight friend, there."

"My burgers are extra-lean ground beef," said Earl. "My French fries are homemade. That sauce in there, it's a family secret."

"Don't let him get to you, Earl," said Alberg, picking up a French fry.

"I make a pretty good spinach salad," said Earl, "but it's nothing, compared to my hamburger."

"Where the hell did you get that thing you're wearing?" said Gillingham.

Proudly, Earl looked down at himself. He was enveloped in a huge white baker's apron. "Paris. Mrs. Eddersley brought it back for me." He returned to the kitchen, tenderly smoothing the apron down over his hips.

Alberg cut his hamburger in half and lifted up the bun so he could sprinkle salt inside. "She went to Strachan's house the day after he died. Said she had to pick up some clothes to bury him in. Found the kid there."

"He'd been there alone all night?"

"I guess so."

"I wonder why he didn't call anybody."

"Probably kept thinking his dad would be home any minute."

"So the next day this aunt shows up and tells him his old man's dead. Must have been a hell of a shock."

"Yeah," said Alberg. He took a bite of his hamburger, leaning over so that his plate would catch the drips.

"This is delicious," said Gillingham, slowly and solemnly, looking into his spinach salad. Then he sighed, and sat back. "Helen Mitchell saw my wife, Marjorie, the other day. My ex-wife, I mean. She says she's lost thirty pounds and dyed her hair. Blond."

Alberg was instantly irate. "Speaking of Helen Mitchell, what the hell do you think you're doing, foisting her off on Cassandra?"

" 'Foisting her off'? Cassandra's her daughter, for God's sake."

"We were supposed to go away," said Alberg sullenly.

Gillingham started to grin. "Oh, my. To Victoria, I bet."

"Yeah. That's right. Thanks a hell of a lot." He took another bite of hamburger. "Marjorie's probably getting married again. To an accountant."

"Your mind is going, Karl," the doctor said calmly. "Marjorie would never in a million years marry an accountant." He brushed fastidiously at some grains of salt sprinkled on the oilcloth that covered the table. "You can't keep Zoe Strachan from burying her brother, you know, just because there's a kid in her house that you don't think ought to be there."

Alberg put the hamburger down. "I've got a real uneasy feeling."

Gillingham snickered. "What is that, a cop's instinct? Kind of your gut reaction sort of thing?"

Alberg leaned his elbows on the table. "When I talked to you this morning, you said something about Strachan not being drunk after all."

"That's right. He'd been drinking, all right. But he wasn't drunk."

Alberg sighed and pushed his plate aside. "I've got a serious problem here. I think you're full of crap about the wounds. 'Not the right kind of wounds.' What the hell does that mean?" He held up his hand. "Just shut up, okay? Until I'm finished. Okay. The guy falls down the stairs. He breaks his neck. He dies. These things happen. She tells us he was drunk. That makes sense. But now you tell me he wasn't drunk." He shrugged. "Okay, so she was wrong. He'd been drinking and he fell down her stairs, so she *assumed* he must have been drunk. I can accept that, too." He leaned forward. "But that kid really bugs me. What the hell is that kid doing there? She doesn't like him. He doesn't like her."

"Okay," said Gillingham agreeably, "so she doesn't like kids. Lots of people don't like kids."

"But why did she haul him home with her, instead of parking him with a friend? A nine-year-old boy, he's bound to have friends he could stay with, people he knows. I just can't figure out why she brought him home with her."

Gillingham looked at him curiously. "I don't know, Karl."

"She's got a hell of a temper," said Alberg softly.

"Are you worried about this kid?" said the doctor after a minute. "I mean, do you think she might hurt him?"

"I don't know," said Alberg slowly. "But I do know that he's scared of her."

"He is?"

"Yeah."

The doctor grunted. "Me, too."

Alberg pulled his plate back in front of him. He picked up his hamburger and immediately put it down again. "What do you mean, you, too?"

"She's colder than a dead fish, that one. Standing at the top of the stairs and laughing like she did." Gillingham shivered.

"She was nervous," said Alberg irritably. "People react strangely in crises. Jesus, you of all people should know that." He picked up his hamburger again, and this time he took a large bite.

Gillingham, munching on spinach, watched his friend closely.

Alberg ate a French fry, but it tasted like cardboard. "We don't have grounds for an inquest, do we?"

Surprised, Gillingham shook his head. "Nope."

"I didn't think so." Alberg slumped back in his chair. "I sure wish I could keep things on hold for a few days. See if I could get a few answers."

Gillingham thought for a while. "She's a foxy lady, isn't she," he said.

Alberg raised his eyebrows. "What? Who?"

"Colder than a dead fish, like I said. But sexy," said the doctor. "Very very sexy."

"What are you getting at, Alex?"

"Maybe you're overreacting."

"What the hell are you talking about?"

Gillingham pointed at him. "That's what I'm talking about. You getting all agitated." He shrugged. "So you want to jump on her bones. So what. So does Sanducci. So did the ambulance guys. You can feel carnal urges and still be a policeman, you know. That's all I meant."

Alberg glowered at him.

"You need a couple of days," Gillingham said thoughtfully, "to sniff around. Satisfy your cop's curiosity. Convince yourself you've done your job." He nodded to himself. "We can get you that. Sure we can."

"How?" said Alberg suspiciously.

Gillingham beamed at him. "We bluff," he said.

"This is not sounding good."

"You go back out there," said the doctor, "and tell her there's some inconclusive findings. Yeah." He leaned forward, all business now. "Okay. Here's my official word, Karl. Are you ready?"

"Go ahead."

"Okay. There's been some inconclusive findings, Staff Sergeant, in the autopsy I performed on the body of the poor soul who plummeted down that Strachan woman's basement steps. I need some more time, to . . . to firm things up, to . . . let's see . . ."

"To complete your work," said Alberg helpfully, "which lies in the area of medical jurisprudence, necessary to the right and proper establishment of the cause and circumstances of the death."

"I couldn't have put it better myself." Gillingham sat back and folded his arms. "That oughta give you a day or two. She might be a tad upset, but what the hell, tell her I'm gonna make sure the process of decay don't get a good grip on him."

CHAPTER

36

When Alberg left her house that morning, Zoe went into her bedroom and changed into jeans and a sweatshirt. She hung up her black skirt and put the green sweater, carefully folded, in a drawer in one of her bedroom closets. Then she went next door, to the spare room.

"I'm going out for a run," she said to the boy, who watched her, big-eyed, from the bed. "I'll be gone for twenty-five minutes."

"How long do I have to stay here?"

"Why did you turn this off?" Zoe switched on the TV set that stood on a low chest of drawers facing the bed. "I don't know how long you have to stay here," she said, and left the room.

It was still raining, but Zoe didn't mind the rain.

She walked briskly down the driveway, in lieu of warming up, and when she reached the highway she began to run.

For the moment I shall put that child from my mind, she

thought; and when I've finished my run, then I'll decide what to do about him.

Cherniak, the family lawyer, would have called the grandparents by now. They could be expected to show up in Sechelt, eventually. But there wasn't anything she could do about that.

She told herself that it wasn't anger she felt. She had gotten her anger under control years before. She was frustrated, that was all. And who could blame her? No wonder she felt frustrated, with that Mountie poking around, disguised as an ordinary person, asking all kinds of questions that were none of his business and then having the monumental effrontery to prevent her from burying her own brother. She wondered if he was going to continue to be a problem, that Mountie.

She was running much faster than usual, virtually pelting along the highway. With an effort she slowed to a jog. Wearing herself out wouldn't accomplish anything except to give her a stitch in the side—which would just make her more irritated.

If she'd been able to follow her plan, she wouldn't be in this mess. If things had gone according to plan, she'd have her scribblers now, and Benjamin would be lying in pieces at the bottom of the cliff. This way, though . . . what a mess, thought Zoe, disgusted, what a blunder, his death half accident and half not. Things had to be planned in order to be made to work. If she'd learned anything in her life by now she'd learned that. Yet in only a minute—no, less than a minute—in seconds, mere seconds of reckless impulse, she'd endangered everything that was important to her. She was extremely frustrated; extremely irritated with herself. But that, she told herself, was wasted energy. Time spent in regret was always time spent inefficiently.

Zoe ran, slowly, steadily, and she thought about her life, and how to protect it.

She had driven into Sechelt on Monday to call Edward Cherniak. It was the first time she'd wished she had a phone of her own. There wasn't a single pay phone in town that was housed in a booth, with a closing door. Most were stuck starkly on the walls of squalid restaurants. She finally found one in the middle of the shopping mall that at least offered a curved sheet of Plexiglas as partial defense against eavesdroppers.

The mall was full of teenagers who ought to have been in school. They lounged against the walls of the mall, bleak eyes staring from pale faces, smoking God knows what and kissing each other. This, she thought grimly, was where that staff sergeant ought to be making himself busy.

"I'm afraid Benjamin is dead," she told Cherniak the lawyer, and waited while he gasped and murmured. "It was an accident. He was drunk, and he fell down my basement stairs." She waited again, through the lawyer's expressions of shock and sorrow. She noticed that several of the teenagers slumped around the vicinity of the telephone wore sharp-toed black boots that looked to be at least three feet long.

"Where's the boy?" said Edward Cherniak. "How is he?"

"He's with me. Has Benjamin got a burial plot?"

Cherniak said, "Yes. Right next to Lorraine."

"Good. I'll let you know as soon as they release the body, so you can make the arrangements."

The lawyer began to protest.

"Oh for heaven's sake, Edward, surely it's one of the things a lawyer does. I have absolutely no wish to get involved in it myself."

A lot of the teenagers, even the boys, had two, three, or more rings in their ears. Zoe thought they looked like people who had been purchased. She shivered with disgust.

"Have you got his will?" she said.

"Yes, of course."

"What's in it?"

"You know I can't tell you that, Zoe. I can't remember anyway. Except that he wanted Peter and Flora Quenneville to have custody of the boy."

"That's fine with me," said Zoe. "I've got another question for you, Edward."

"Of course."

"Did Benjamin ever leave anything with you? A package? Something he wanted you to keep for him?" Portions of the teenagers' heads were shaven, and the hair that remained was dyed bizarre colors, like fuchsia, and lime green, and lifeless black.

"A package," said the lawyer. "No. I don't think so. No, I'm sure of it. Why?"

"Has he got a safe-deposit box somewhere?"

"I have no idea, Zoe. Why?"

"He had something of mine. I want it back."

She'd hung up, then, and placed another call, this time to Benjamin's West Vancouver bank, where her brother had a safe-deposit box, all right. But there was no way they were going to let her see what was in it.

Furious, she'd crashed the receiver down onto the hook and whirled away from the phone.

"Hey, lady," said a lethargic young male person wearing faded jeans stuffed into black boots, and a worn black leather jacket over a black T-shirt with lettering on it; Zoe could read only two words: "suck blood." She stopped and stared at him. "Hey, can you give me some money?"

Zoe gazed at him, incredulous. "Are you out of your mind?" she said. "Get out of my way, or I'll have you arrested."

"For what?" he said, plaintively, to her retreating back.

Now, the next day, she ran, and ran, in the hope that physical activity would wear off some of her frustration and prevent anger from happening.

She had built herself a refuge. It had been her father's idea.

Zoe ran easily, her legs pumping, her heart beating fast. It was gratifying to have confidence in your body, she thought.

She liked the Douglas fir trees that clustered around the guest cottage and lined the edge of her property, because they protected her privacy. She liked the arbutus because the bark peeled away to reveal shiny red skin, and their leaves didn't fall, even though they looked like the leaves of deciduous trees.

She liked it that her living room and study faced west, onto the patio. She enjoyed the fact that the other side of the house had no windows. She took great pleasure in the large amount of storage space in the basement, and often in her head ticked off the things she had packed away down there: case lots of canned foods and paper products, kerosene lamps and plenty of fuel, boxes of candles and matches, dozens of large plastic bottles of spring water.

It was comforting to have plenty of money.

Yes, she thought, running toward the Sitka spruce that loomed ahead, at the halfway point in her run, all in all it was very satisfying indeed to have achieved so perfect a life.

She couldn't have done it without her father.

She reached the spruce tree, pressed the palm of her right hand against its trunk, then pressed the palm of her left hand there, and then she turned around and ran back toward her house.

Her father was a geologist and had made some shrewd mining investments. But the thing that brought him real wealth was his own mine, Great North, which he bought and developed over more than ten years with his two brothers, who were also geologists. By the time she graduated from high school, Zoe knew that her financial future was secured; her father had made it a point to assure her of this. And later, she realized why, and understood that she had been fortunate in her parentage.

She was indisputably intelligent, and capable of working hard. But she was also quickly bored, and when she was bored, hard work was impossible. She entered university but dropped out before Christmas in her first year. She then had a succession of jobs but couldn't keep any of them—didn't want to keep any of them. Her parents, especially her mother, complained about this but continued to support her. They refused to support her in her own apartment, however, until she became twenty-one.

Zoe knew that if she hadn't been able to depend on her father for money, she would have had to figure some way to steal. This would have made for a turbulent and disorderly life. She was glad that it hadn't been necessary.

It was hardly raining at all now, she noticed as she neared

the turnoff to her driveway. She left the highway and slowed to a walk, cooling down.

She had gone from job to job, and apartment to apartment, during the years that her parents remained alive, and gradually learned what things gave her pleasure, what circumstances repressed her anger, what activities were capable of absorbing her attention.

Her father watched her learn these things, and it was he who spoke to her about constructing for herself a sanctuary. Zoe had liked this notion very much.

When they died, first her father, then her mother, she quit her current job, invested her inheritance shrewdly, and retired eventually to the Sunshine Coast.

She glanced at the guesthouse as she passed it, and wondered when she'd need it again. It had been six months since the last time.

But what with one thing and another, she thought, panting, striding toward her house, it was liable to be quite a while before she felt hungry for sex again.

Inside, she stripped and showered and put on her black skirt and green sweater again.

Then she went to the spare room.

"Come into the kitchen," she said. "I want to talk to you while I make lunch."

"I could stay with Roddy," he said in the kitchen.

Zoe opened a can of chicken noodle soup, added a can of water, and set it on the stove to warm. "We have to have a funeral for your father."

He slid down the wall until he was squatting.

"I didn't find what I was looking for in your house," said Zoe, getting a loaf of bread out of the cupboard. She fetched tomatoes and lettuce from the fridge and began making sandwiches. "Where else should I look?" He didn't answer. She looked at him and saw that he'd hunched up his shoulders so that he looked as if he had no neck.

"I live here," he'd said, after nearly scaring the wits out of her. And it had turned out to be true.

She'd sat him in a chair where she could keep an eye on him and told him to stay put. Then she locked the door, pocketed the key, and set about searching Benjamin's study. She searched the desk, the filing cabinets, the bookshelves. Her hands became grimy and sticky. She searched for an hour; two hours; three. The back of her neck was sweaty under her hair. She felt as if she were smothering under the weight of somebody else's life—and she found not a trace of her scribblers.

She learned that since the death of Benjamin's wife the house had been mortgaged and mortgaged and mortgaged again. That stocks had been sold, bonds had been sold, retirement savings plans given up for cash.

And she learned that seven years earlier, Benjamin and Lorraine had adopted a two-year-old child.

There were also files filled with spotty correspondence with employers and potential employers. Benjamin had been working for the same firm for four years when the adoption was approved, and remained with the company until a year after Lorraine's death, when he'd been "regretfully" dismissed because of chronic absenteeism. Since then he'd had several jobs and lost them all. The most recent letter in the file, though, was only a few months old. It welcomed Benjamin to a firm of chartered accountants located in an address at the corner of Burrard and Hastings.

"Your father had a new job," Zoe had said to the boy sitting in the chair.

He nodded.

She'd stood up then, stretching, and looked at her watch. She had to leave right away to catch the last ferry.

She stared at the boy, thinking. "You'd better come with me," she said abruptly.

"I could stay with Roddy," he'd said.

And now he was saying it again.

"I told you," said Zoe, slapping the tomato-and-lettuce sandwiches together. "We have to have a funeral for your father."

"When?"

"Soon."

She poured herself some coffee, put the plate of sandwiches on the table, and ladled chicken soup into bowls. "Sit down," she said. "Eat lunch."

Kenny sat down. He cringed when she set the bowl of soup in front of him. "For heaven's sake, what's the matter with you? Did Benjamin beat you or something?"

He shook his head.

"Then stop that damned flinching. Eat." Zoe picked up a sandwich. "I was looking for something very important," she said to the boy.

He had pale-brown hair and large hazel eyes, and he was thin; a homely child, she thought. She didn't like the way he kept looking at her, hardly blinking, as if any second she might pounce on him.

"It's something that belongs to me," said Zoe. She took a bite of the sandwich. "Your father borrowed it," she said, her mouth full of white bread, margarine, mayonnaise, tomato. "I went to get it back." She dabbed at the edges of her mouth with a paper napkin. "Eat," she said to the boy, who hadn't moved.

She waited until his hand crept across the table and took hold of a soup spoon. Then she waited some more, until he'd eaten several spoonfuls. She nodded, relieved. She couldn't have him starve to death, after all, right here in her house.

"Scribblers," she said. "That's what I was looking for."

Kenny bent his head and continued spooning the soup into his mouth.

"Don't slurp," said Zoe. "It's very rude."

He ate, rapidly, shoulders hunched.

Zoe watched him, thinking.

She reached out and grabbed his shoulder. "Look at me." Kenny shoveled more soup into his mouth. The spoon scraped against the bottom of the bowl. Zoe shook him, and he dropped the spoon. "Look at me." He looked at her, not into her eyes but at her mouth. "You know about them."

He shook his head, staring at her mouth.

"You do," said Zoe softly. "You do."

Both of them heard the sound of automobile tires crunching the gravel outside Zoe's front door.

CHAPTER

37

The door was flung open wide, and Zoe Strachan stood there glaring at him.

"Hey," said Alberg. He lifted his hands, palms out. "Whatever it is, I didn't do it."

She made an effort to relax. "Hello again, Staff Sergeant," she said.

"I've spoken to Dr. Gillingham."

"Good."

"But he can't release the body just yet. I'm sorry."

She looked at him steadily, and her cheeks flushed the palest pink imaginable; it was almost imperceptible. But he thought he could feel the surge in her blood pressure.

"May I come in?" said Alberg. "I'll try to explain." Yeah, right, he thought. It had been dawning on him for some time that he had not sufficiently prepared himself for this conversation.

"Where's the boy?" he said, as he followed her to the living room.

"He's in his room." She sat in the black leather chair near the window. She didn't look very hospitable. It would have been better, he thought, if she'd had a phone.

"I wouldn't want him to hear us," said Alberg.

"He won't hear us. He's watching television."

Alberg sat on the sofa. "There are some—the autopsy results are inconclusive," he said. He was appalled to realize that the palms of his hands were sweating.

"I find that extremely hard to believe," said Zoe. She crossed her legs. "The man fell down the stairs. He struck his head on the concrete floor. He died. There was nothing inconclusive about it. I was there."

Alberg glanced into the hall, but he couldn't see the door to Kenny's room from where he sat.

"The boy is very upset," said Zoe Strachan. "And you're not helping matters any. He can't even begin to recover until there's been a funeral." Her cheeks had grown more pink, and her eyes were bright.

"The problem is—he's thinking about asking for an inquest," Alberg said quickly, before he could change his mind. "Dr. Gillingham is."

She stared at him, astonished. "What on earth for?"

"Well, he has some questions. . . ." Alberg stood up, his mind racing in fruitless circles. "This is very difficult, Miss Strachan."

She watched him. "I can't imagine why."

"The alcohol content in his blood was negligible," said Alberg, blundering on. "That is to say, he wasn't drunk." His mind was hollering at him to get out of there fast, stop babbling and get the hell out.

"Well, really," said Zoe. She stood up. "Who's in a better position to know whether he was drunk or not—some doctor who never met the man alive, or the person who was there when he died?"

"I'd have to go with the doctor, ma'am," said Alberg. He felt completely unnerved. It was humiliating.

Hands on her hips, she gave him a hostile look. "What are you saying, Staff Sergeant? Do you suspect me of murdering my brother?"

Alberg tried to think, distracted by her body, by her presence, by the sweat that was now breaking out under his arms. "What I'm saying, what the doctor suggests as a possibility—" He didn't have the faintest idea what was going to come out of his mouth next. "—and it's only a possibility, remember—" Frantically, he tried to recall whether Gillingham had in fact suggested anything useful at all. "—what the facts suggest, you see, is that since he wasn't intoxicated, perhaps, then, he didn't fall; perhaps, instead, he—he—"

"Pitched himself down the stairs on purpose?" said Zoe, incredulous.

"Well, now," said Alberg, "not exactly, no." Do something, for God's sake, he told himself. Get on the offensive. "Probably not," he said. "But after all, you didn't actually see him fall," he said.

"I—what do you mean?"

"You were here, weren't you? In the living room."

"Well, yes, but—"

"And you heard a crash."

"Yes."

"Now, he went downstairs for a bottle of wine, is that right?"

"That's right."

What the hell was he doing? This wouldn't accomplish anything—it was too easy to explain away. Alberg, he thought, furious, you're an idiot.

"Did he fall on his way down?" he said.

"He certainly didn't fall *up* the stairs, Staff Sergeant."

"I mean," said Alberg, "did he fall when he was going down, or when he was coming up?"

"I haven't the faintest idea."

"Think about it," he said. "How much time elapsed? He left the living room, you heard a yell; how much time passed in between?"

She stalked over to the window and stood with her back to him, looking out at the gray, drizzly day. "I do not understand why you insist on making things difficult for me."

"There was a bottle of wine on your kitchen counter," said Alberg.

There. He'd said it.

"Why was there a bottle of wine in your kitchen?" he said gently.

She turned to face him, taking her time. She tilted her head and looked quizzical. He couldn't tell. He didn't have a bloody clue what was going on in her head.

"I don't understand the question," she said.

"Your brother went down into the basement to get some wine." He wasn't going to get a damn thing from her. "But there was a bottle already up here, in your kitchen."

"Was there?" She walked past him, back to the black leather chair. She walked so close to him that he felt the air stir.

He nodded. "Unless that was the bottle he went down to get." He watched her thinking about this. He felt boundlessly patient. "But that wouldn't make sense, would it?" She just looked at him, still thinking. "If he fell on his way down, he wouldn't have had a bottle." Zoe nodded, slowly. "If he fell on his way up, the bottle would surely have broken." She nodded again. "So you see my problem."

"Oh, I don't think it's a problem, Staff Sergeant," she said. "There's a very simple explanation, actually."

He nodded. "Okay."

"I forgot, that's all. I forgot there was a bottle in the kitchen." She pushed her hair away from her temples. "I am a forgetful person. From time to time."

Alberg looked into her face and saw blue eyes and pale smooth skin and a luscious mouth, and he knew that she was lying. He was filled with relief. He gave her a sunny smile. "I'd like to see Kenny now, please."

Zoe clasped her hands in front of her and called, loudly, "Kenny." She watched Alberg closely, curiously, while they waited for the boy.

He stood up when Kenny sidled into the room, and held out his hand. "Hi, Kenny," he said. The child hesitated, then awkwardly shook hands. "Sit down." The boy sat on the edge of the wing chair near the doorway to the hall. "Do you think we could have some coffee?" Alberg asked Zoe.

"This isn't a social occasion," she snapped. "And I'm not anybody's waitress."

This won't do, thought Zoe, horrified. Where was her self-control? She couldn't afford to lose control.

She inhaled, slowly, deeply, and told her body to relax. "I beg your pardon," she said quietly. "That wasn't very hospitable."

Alberg smiled at her. She let his smile penetrate her skin. "It's all right," he said. "I drink too much coffee anyway."

He moved to the end of the sofa so as to be closer to the boy. "I want to ask you some questions, Kenny. Okay?"

"About my dad?" The boy's glance flickered around the room; Zoe felt it bounce off her face like a bird against a windowpane. "People don't know he's dead yet, do they?" he said.

"What do you mean?" said Alberg.

"Roddy doesn't know it. Roddy's my best friend." He was picking at the fabric of the chair with thin, nervous fingers. "I could stay with him, I bet. He probably wonders where I am."

"Maybe you could phone him," said Alberg.

"She doesn't have a phone," said Kenny. "And I don't think Grandma and Grandpa know, either," he said, picking away.

Zoe bit the inside of her mouth to prevent herself from telling him to leave the damn chair alone. It was exceedingly difficult to concentrate on the policeman with this wretched child in the room.

"Your grandma and grandpa—where do they live?" said Alberg, getting a notebook and pen from his inside jacket pocket.

"In Winnipeg," said Kenny. He tucked his hands into his armpits. "We went to see them once. But usually they come to see us."

"What's their last name, Kenny, do you know?"

"Sure I know. It's Quenneville. Grandpa's first name is Peter, and Grandma's first name is . . . I forget."

"I'll phone them from the police station," said Alberg. "I'll phone Roddy, too, if you like."

"Yeah, that'd be good. I know his number. I phone him all the time."

Alberg wrote down the number in his notebook. "I'll do it right away," he said. "And I'll come back tomorrow to give you a report."

Kenny stood up. "I could go and stay with him. Maybe his dad would come and get me."

"Maybe you can do that after the funeral," said Zoe. She turned to Alberg and offered him a faint smile—but she felt awkward, uncertain; she was furious with the boy for somehow robbing her of grace and confidence.

"Flora," said Kenny. "Grandma's name is Flora."

"Okay," said Alberg. "Got it." He stood up to leave.

"Can I come with you?" said the boy.

"You'd better stay with me, I think," said Zoe, making her voice soft, "until your grandparents come for you." She got up and went over to stand behind him, one hand on his head in what she hoped looked like a gesture of affection. "I'm quite sure they'll come for you, once the staff sergeant has spoken to them. Aren't you, Staff Sergeant?"

His face was suddenly closed to her. She felt a spasm of irritation. Then he winked, and she was dumbfounded, then furious.

"I'll be back," he said to the boy. "Tomorrow."

"Promise?"

"I promise," said Alberg, his eyes on Zoe.

CHAPTER
38

Alberg returned to the detachment, to find the place reeking of vinegar and the waiting room choked with elderly persons, some of whom appeared hostile.

"You should use the back door sometimes," said Isabella.

"What the hell's all this?" muttered Alberg. "Who're these people?"

"They're here to see you. If you'd use the back door sometimes," she said again, as a few of the visitors began ominously shuffling their feet, "I could deal with this kind of thing better."

"Where's Sid?" said Alberg. "I can't handle this now. I've got to make a phone call."

"One of them is Horace Orlitzki," said Isabella. "Ramona's boy. Come all the way from Cache Creek."

"Oh, shit."

"Excuse me, sir." A man of about seventy-five approached the counter. He was white-haired and elegant, and reminded

Alberg of the late Duke of Windsor. "These ladies and gentlemen are a delegation from the Seniors. I'm their spokesman. Bernard Rundle." He held out his hand. "It's about Mrs. Orlitzki."

"Good to meet you, Mr. Rundle," said Alberg, shaking hands. "Excuse me for a minute. Isabella?"

She followed him into his office.

"Isabella. Dammit. You're supposed to have gone home by now. Instead of that, you've been doing the damn blinds again. The whole place stinks of vinegar."

"That's right. And the windows. I also gave your desk a good polish."

"But we have somebody else to do the cleaning around here. You weren't hired as a damn cleaning lady."

"It seems to me," she said sharply, "you ought to put your mind to those folks out there, instead of to who's a cleaning lady and who's not. They're worried about Ramona, just like I am. So they come to find out from you what's going on. What do you plan to tell them, anyway?"

"I told you, for God's sake, I can't deal with this now. I've got to make a phone call."

Isabella hesitated. "It's better when I'm here," she said quietly. "Right on top of things. Keeping myself busy."

Alberg sighed. "I know, Isabella. I know. How long have they been waiting?"

"The old people just got here not ten minutes ago. Horace Orlitzki's been in and out for the past hour."

"Okay. Send him in. And then Mr. Rundle. If Sid shows up, I want to see him, too."

Horace Orlitzki was a tall, balding man in his early forties, with a cherubic face and soft, puffy hands. He wore a plaid blazer over navy-blue trousers.

"My sister Martha and I, we're going to hire us a PI," he told Alberg.

"A what?"

"A PI. Private investigator. We want to get this thing settled, once and for all."

"What thing is that, Mr. Orlitzki?"

"It's my understanding, a body could be swept away by the tide, buried by a mudslide, any number of things, you're not going to come across it in the normal course of events."

"Excuse me. Are you talking about your mother?"

Orlitzki nodded. "She can't be declared legally dead, it's my understanding, until a certain amount of time has passed."

"Right."

"So we're going to hire us a PI, and he's going to find the body. Put our minds to rest. Who can you recommend?"

"Who can I recommend?"

"Money. It'll cost us. We know that."

"Let me get this straight. You want to hire a private cop to find your mother's body."

"That's it. You got it."

"What if he finds her alive?"

"Pardon?"

"What if she isn't dead?"

Orlitzki shook his head. "I don't follow you."

Alberg stood up, went to his door, and opened it. "Isabella!" he hollered. He turned to Horace Orlitzki. "I don't know any PIs," he said. "Try the Vancouver yellow pages."

"But—"

"Mr. Orlitzki. You look for your mother dead. We'll go on looking for her alive. Isabella!"

Orlitzki scooted off, muttering imprecations, and Isabella

appeared, with Bernard Rundle in tow and Sid Sokolowski trundling along behind.

"Sid," said Alberg. "Good. Mr. Rundle, I tell you what, you'll be better off talking to Sergeant Sokolowski, here. He's in charge of the case. Sid, this is Mr. Rundle. He represents some of Ramona's friends. They're anxious to know how things are progressing. Would you fill him in?"

Alone in his office, he closed the door and called Gillingham.

"Those wounds on Strachan," he said to the doctor. "The head, the gut. Could either of them have been inflicted by a bottle? A wine bottle?"

CHAPTER
39

"I've got some business to do today," his dad had told him, "and I might be late getting home."

"Is it your new job?" said Kenny.

His dad put on that big smile that Kenny loved. "No," he said, reaching over to mess up Kenny's hair. "It's something else."

His dad had said he'd be back by dinnertime, and he was.

He was feeling really good when he got home, too. For supper he made Kenny's favorite thing, macaroni and cheese, and a salad, and he sent Kenny to the store on his bike to get some buns.

His dad got kind of drunk on the wine he drank with his dinner, but not a lot drunk, and he stayed happy and boisterous, which made Kenny feel good.

After Kenny had been in bed for a while he heard a tap on his door. It opened a little bit, and his dad said, "Ken? You awake?" He came in and sat on the edge of Kenny's bed.

"Things are going to be a lot better from now on," he said, pulling awkwardly at the comforter, trying to get it up over Kenny's shoulders. "I've been worried about money, you know?"

Kenny nodded. He knew, all right.

"But everything's going to be okay now." His dad patted Kenny's cheek. "We're going to be rich again." He got up and sort of staggered, and held on to the edge of the doorway and laughed. "Been too deep into the old vino," he said. "But that's going to be okay, too, Ken," he said, sounding serious, churchlike. He put his finger across his lips. "Shhh. I want to show you something. Don't go away." He went down the hall toward his bedroom.

Kenny put his hands behind his head and waited.

After a while his dad came back, and he was carrying something. He sat down on Kenny's bed again. "See these?" Kenny watched his dad pull three small, dog-eared exercise books, one yellow, and one red, and one blue, out of a brown envelope. The covers had faded, and the corners were scrunched.

"They don't look like much," said his dad, "but they're worth a lot of money, Ken. A whole lot of money." He squeezed his eyes shut tight, and his mouth, too, and his whole body shook for a while, trying to hold in his laughter. After a minute he kind of relaxed, and sighed, and opened his eyes. "I want you to look after them for me for a while. A few days." He stood up, groping for the wall. He leaned against it and looked around Kenny's room. "Where's a good hiding place, Ken?"

"Why do you need to hide them?" said Kenny.

His dad frowned up at the ceiling. "I probably don't. But I'm going to do it anyway. So where's a good place?"

Kenny had shown him the hole in his closet where the wall was a little bit bashed in. His dad put the exercise books back in the brown envelope and put the envelope in the hole.

"Good," he'd said, scrambling unsteadily to his feet. "Good." He took Kenny by the shoulders. "Don't tell anybody they're in there," he said, sounding solemn and mysterious. "Not anybody. Promise?" And Kenny had promised.

Two days later his dad went away on business again. This time he didn't get home for supper. Kenny waited and waited. He waited all night long. And into the next day. And his dad didn't come home, and he didn't phone, nobody phoned, and Kenny was scared to use the telephone, in case his dad tried to call, and he was scared to leave the house, and scared to stay, but he stayed anyway, waiting for his dad, and his dad didn't come but then his Aunt Zoe did, and she told him that his dad was dead.

At first Kenny didn't believe her.

But then he did.

When she told him to pack his pajamas he did, he packed them in his gym bag, along with some other stuff, and he looked around for a photograph of his dad to take with him, but he couldn't find one.

He put on his oversize ski jacket with all the big pockets, and into one of the inside pockets he put the brown envelope, because he couldn't leave it behind in case somebody—a prowler or a thief or just somebody like a bad kid—got into the empty house and found it.

That had been days ago.

Kenny didn't know why he hadn't told his Aunt Zoe right away at lunchtime that he had what she was looking for.

Because she scared him, that was why. Partly why.

He waited long into the night, until he was absolutely sure there wasn't a single sound happening anywhere in the house. Then he got the flashlight from his gym bag, and the brown envelope from his pocket, and he climbed into bed, pulled the covers over his head and slid out the exercise books. He opened the one on top and the first thing he saw, printed in big letters, was his aunt's name. Kenny began to read.

CHAPTER
40

Early Wednesday morning, Ramona pulled the curtain back and looked outside into fog. It swirled lazily around vague, dark, vertical shapes that she knew were the trunks of the fir trees that surrounded the cottage. Her heart gladdened as she peered out into the fog; there was brightness behind it, and when it lifted she knew there would be sunshine. She couldn't see the branches of the trees, or the ferns and salal that grew close to the ground; only the dark poles of the trunks, which seemed to emerge out of fog and vanish into fog, as though the trees had no branches, and were not rooted in the earth. Ramona heard a vibrant, insistent birdcall, one note, sweeping upward, repeated again and again, one voice calling into the fog, maybe seeing beyond it, to the sun.

She turned from the window and got herself dressed.

In the kitchen she made a small pencil mark on the cupboard door, next to three similar marks; in this way she was keeping track of the length of her stay. Then she ate two crackers and a handful of macadamia nuts, and drank a small bottle of an Australian substance that was apparently watered-down fruit juice.

Ramona desperately craved real juice, real fruit. She had even started dreaming about fruit, about Golden Delicious apples with a pink flush on them; huge navel oranges, thick skinned, dripping with sweetness like nectar; bananas, cool and yielding; not pineapple, too much acid, but nectarines . . . peaches . . . strawberries . . . she clutched the countertop and gave a little moan. She was going to have to get herself some fruit somehow, somewhere, no two ways about it.

When she'd finished her breakfast she crept out of the cottage, closing the door softly, after making sure it wasn't going to lock behind her.

The air was moist and sticky, and it smelled like spring. Ramona waded through fog into the shelter of the trees. She felt wonderfully joyous, and tried to give one of the trees a hug, but she couldn't get her arms all the way around its trunk. She rubbed her cheek gently against the rough bark and smelled the spicy fragrance of the branches rustling up there above her. She saw a flash of bright blue and heard the indignant, raucous cry of a Stellar's jay and wondered what had happened to her bird book: she kept it handy by the window all the time, with a pair of binoculars right next to it; she used the binoculars mostly for looking at things out on the water, various kinds of boats and so forth, but it was useful for birds, too. My goodness, she thought, dazed, clinging to the fir tree, I don't know where the ocean is.

Ramona hung on tight, waiting. The fog was dense, and suffocating. It was malevolent; it seemed to mock her. She felt threatened, panicky, but she kept on waiting, waiting, not knowing what she was waiting for, obeying some instruction she couldn't remember getting . . . and then, abruptly, she knew again where she was. Who she was.

It was like having somebody stop sitting on your chest, she thought, as she hung on to the tree, panting slightly. It was like pushing with all your might against an immovable object, which suddenly gives way. Losing yourself, then finding you again.

She felt a flood of terror that made her start to sweat.

She thought about going into town for fruit, and library books, and having lunch with Isabella, and at the end of the day going to bed in the hospital.

Ramona pushed herself slowly away from the fir tree and rubbed her arms. She'd had a week. And it was a week she'd never expected to have. She was very glad she'd taken it.

She wondered how the nurses would react, when she walked back in there, bold as brass.

She fastened the top button of her coat, shook her head wearily, and headed toward the driveway.

When she got there she stood still, uncertain because of the fog which way to start walking, and then she realized that she had changed her mind.

She wasn't ready to go back, after all. Not just yet.

She left the driveway and sat down on the damp ground, leaning against a tree. What's the worst thing that could happen to me? she asked herself.

She could forget she'd put something on the stove to heat and end up setting fire to the place.

She flinched, thinking about it; she'd done it twice now. She hadn't set fire to the place, but she'd completely forgotten the pot on the stove, until it boiled over. She had been certain that such a thing couldn't happen again, but it *had* happened again, the very next day.

All right, she told herself, what to do about that is easy. I'll stop using the stove, that's all. I'll unplug it from the wall, is what I'll do.

Now, what else bad could happen?

She felt a sickening lurch of dread and tried to turn away from it but couldn't, and finally she said, out loud, "I could forget what I'm doing and where I am. And this time not ever get myself back again."

Ramona leaned back against the treetrunk. Obviously she'd be a lot better off in the hospital, when that happened, *if* it happened, than out wandering around the world on her own. All right, she thought, what would I want to happen, if I forgot who I was when I was out in the world on my own?

She would want somebody to take her back to the hospital, to Dr. Gillingham.

She thought, what can I do to make sure that what I want to happen happens?

She could write a note explaining her situation and pin it to the front of her coat.

But what if her memory vanished while she was in bed?

She'd write several notes, she decided, and pin one on her coat, one on the sweater she always wore, and one on Marcia's nightgown that she'd borrowed. It would be damned humiliating, going around wearing notes all the time, but it was protection, necessary protection. Against herself.

She hauled herself wearily to her feet and glanced up the driveway toward where she knew the big house stood, shrouded now in fog and sea mist. She wondered if the Strachan woman might go out today, and leave her door unlocked, for once. She was bound to have fresh fruit on hand, a fitness-type person like that, going jogging all the time.

Ramona became aware of a sound: not a bird, not the nearby ocean, not a genial breeze come to sweep away the fog. She tilted her head, concentrating, and watched, and waited, wondering why she wasn't trying to hide herself.

A shape began to materialize, and Ramona saw that it was a small boy, hurrying. He was enveloped in a large jacket and had something clutched to his chest. He didn't see her as he scurried along; he was looking down intently, as if afraid the ground would disappear if he didn't keep an eye on it.

"Hello," said Ramona, and the boy skittered sideways, away from the sound of her voice, and spotted her standing in the fog on the edge of the driveway, and stopped in his tracks.

When Kenny had finished reading the scribblers, he switched off his flashlight and lay for a long time in the dark, under the covers. He couldn't hear anything except his heart, which was beating so fast that he thought it might be trying to pound its way right out of his chest.

He had to get out of there.

But he was too scared to move.

He'd have to move, though, because he had to get out of there, that was for sure.

After a while he pulled the covers down, very slowly, about two inches. Nothing happened, so he pulled them down some more, and eventually he was peering over the top of them.

The room was totally black. Kenny blinked his eyes. Soon he could see shapes. He held his breath and listened, but he couldn't hear anything except for the muffled sound of the ocean.

He wished very much that he could pull the covers back over his head and just stay there, invisible, until his dad came to rescue him. He felt himself starting to cry.

I've got to make a plan, he thought, and remembered the ten dollars his dad had given him the morning he left. "If I'm not back by the time you get home from school, buy yourself a pizza," his dad had said. But Kenny had decided to wait for his dad before ordering the pizza, and his dad never came, so Kenny still had the ten dollars. That ought to be enough to pay for the ferry ride, he thought.

Very carefully, he crawled out of bed and tiptoed around the room collecting his stuff, hunched over, hardly breathing. He put his things in the gym bag, leaving behind the clothes his Aunt Zoe had bought for him. . . . He shivered, and pushed her out of his mind.

He got dressed, slowly, quietly; he'd never been so quiet in his life. Then he put on his jacket and sat down on the floor by the window to wait for the sky to get a little bit light.

It was a long way to the ferry. But he could walk there anyway, he knew he could. Maybe somebody would offer him a ride for part of the way. Maybe he could hitchhike. But people didn't like seeing kids hitchhiking. They'd probably ask a lot of questions about where he was going and where he lived and did his dad know he was hitchhiking. So that wouldn't be a good idea. But if he was just walking along looking like he wasn't worried about anything, somebody might stop, then, and offer him a ride, and since he hadn't asked for it, it would be okay to take it. And when he got across on the ferry to Horseshoe Bay he'd phone Roddy, and maybe he could go and stay with him, maybe Roddy's dad would even drive to Horseshoe Bay to get him, because it was a long walk from Horseshoe Bay to West Vancouver, too.

Kenny wiped the tears from his face and wished he could stop crying but at least it was quiet crying; he wasn't making any noise at all.

"I didn't mean to scare you," said the old lady.

Kenny held on tightly to his gym bag.

"It's going to be a nice day," she said.

Kenny's eyes flickered right and left.

"The fog'll burn away, oh, about noon, maybe sooner."

Kenny gave her a quick glance, then looked down the driveway, toward where he thought the highway was.

"Where are you off to?" she said.

"Home."

She nodded. "And where might that be?"

"I don't have to tell you anything," said Kenny quickly.

"That's right. You don't."

He started moving away.

"Can I ask you a favor?" she said.

"I've gotta go," said Kenny.

"If anybody asks you if you've seen me, will you please tell them no?"

Kenny stopped. "Why?"

"Can you keep a secret?"

Reluctantly, Kenny nodded.

"I ran away."

Kenny frowned. "From where?"

"A place where they keep old people."

"What do you mean," said Kenny, skeptical, "a place where they keep old people?"

"I went back to my own house. But they came looking for me there. So now," she said, spreading her hands, "I'm staying here."

"In the woods?" said Kenny.

She hesitated, then pointed across the driveway.

Kenny turned and peered through the fog. "Where? What?"

"There's a little house there."

Kenny walked close enough to be able to see it. Then he went back to the driveway. He stared at the old lady. She looked weird, with that big old coat, and her gray hair all tangled. But her face was calm and friendly. She looked weird, but she didn't look like a crazy person. His Aunt Zoe, now, *she* was a crazy person. But his Aunt Zoe didn't look weird at all. "Did you really run away?" he asked the old lady.

"Yes, I did." She looked off into space, figuring something. "I believe it was just one week ago," she said.

"Are the people who're looking for you—are they mad at you?"

"I don't think so. I think they're probably just worried about me."

Kenny nodded. "Yeah. My dad, he'd've worried, if I'd've run away." He hugged the gym bag tight. "He died, though."

"Who, your dad?"

Kenny nodded.

"That's terrible," said the old lady.

Kenny heard in the distance a quick crunching noise. He looked into the fog, straining to see. Oh please God help me, he said inside his head, and he dropped the gym bag onto the ground and fumbled with the zipper. "Here," he said to the old lady, thrusting the brown envelope toward her. "Oh please hide this. Please hide it."

The old lady took the brown envelope from his out-stretched hand. She looked puzzled, and started to say something, but then he could see in her face that she was hearing the crunching noise too, and she didn't speak, she listened, hard. The noise was getting a lot louder . . . and then suddenly his Aunt Zoe emerged out of the whiteness with fear on her face that turned to relief, and then anger, when she saw him.

"What do you think you're doing?" she said to him in a furious whisper, as though she didn't want to talk loudly in the fog.

He looked quickly at the old lady; but she wasn't there anymore.

"Where do you think you're going?" said his aunt, taking him by the arm.

He wondered if she'd been there at all.

His Aunt Zoe propelled him around and back up the driveway, towards the house. Kenny looked backward over his shoulder but he couldn't see the old lady, he couldn't see anything but the swirling fog.

CHAPTER

41

Alberg woke early Wednesday morning. He lay with his hands behind his head, staring up at the ceiling of his bedroom. It was still dark outside, and he could see only dimly. The cats were sleeping at the end of his bed, entwined like lovers. Alberg lay quietly, shuffling his thoughts, trying to make sense of them.

"Sure," Gillingham had said. "A wine bottle could've done it. Either one. The head wound. The bruise on the stomach. But so could a lot of other things, much as I hate to tell you this yet again. Including, as you yourself pointed out, falling down the damn stairs."

It was pure bad luck that the fall had killed him, thought Alberg. He might easily have just broken a leg, or an arm—or nothing at all. As a method of committing murder, shoving somebody down the stairs left a great deal to be desired.

But if it was an accident, why had she lied about the wine bottle?

All right, he thought. Say she did it. *How* did she do it?

Her brother's standing at the top of the stairs. He's going to go down to get the wine. He says something, who knows what, that makes her mad; she loses her cool and heaves him down. Unluckily for her, he dies. She decides to pretend it was an accident. Which it almost was, thought Alberg, if in fact that's the way it happened.

Or: She planned it out. Lured him to her house, bopped him on the head with the wine bottle, then threw him down the stairs to make it look like an accident.

But why, for Christ's sake?

Alberg sat up in bed. He rubbed his scalp vigorously. No bloody way he could ever prove anything, if he hadn't decided what to believe himself.

And what's all this speculation got to do with the boy? With her anger toward the boy, and his apparent fear of her?

"I need more information," he muttered. He peered at his bedside clock. Six-thirty. Eight-thirty in Winnipeg. He reached for the phone.

He'd tried several times the previous evening to call Kenny's grandparents, but the line was continually busy. This morning, though, he got through.

It turned out that they already knew about Benjamin Strachan's death. Strachan's lawyer, who'd gotten the news from Zoe, had called them Monday afternoon.

"He told us Kenny's with his aunt," said Peter Quenneville. "Of course we want to talk to him. But the phone company keeps on telling me she doesn't have a phone, if you can believe that. I was just getting to my wits' end, here. I was just getting it in my head to call you people, as a matter of fact."

"He's okay," said Alberg. "But I know he'd like to talk to

you. I'll tell Miss Strachan to get him to a phone this afternoon."

"We're coming out there," said Kenny's grandfather. "The wife won't fly. We'll get the train out of here tomorrow; it'll land us in Vancouver Saturday, supposedly at ten in the morning, but it's always late. So hold off on the funeral till then, will you? And listen," he said, not waiting for a reply. "Tell Kenny not to worry, his granddad's on his way. Tell him that."

Alberg imagined him tall and sturdy, with a straight back and a lot of thick white hair. "I'll tell him, Mr. Quenneville. By the way. Have you ever met Zoe Strachan?"

"Never," said Peter Quenneville. "Never met her. Why? What's she like?"

Alberg hesitated. "Cold," he said finally. "She's . . . cold."

"It figures. It figures. Goddammit. Isn't there somebody else Kenny can stay with? Until we get there?"

"Maybe," said Alberg, reaching for his notepad and pen, which were on his night table. "I'll see what I can do. Meanwhile, can you give me the name of the lawyer who called you? And his number?"

Kenny's grandfather did so.

"Thanks," said Alberg. "What can you tell me about the boy's aunt, Mr. Quenneville? Did Benjamin ever talk about her?" He started drawing a picture of a train in his notebook.

"Not much, Mr. Alberg." He sighed, and Alberg heard a squeaking sound, probably as Peter Quenneville sat down. Alberg figured he was talking from the kitchen of his house. His wife would be nearby, listening worriedly. "I liked Benjamin, you know. But he was woolly-headed, a bit of a dreamer; he had a hard time holding a job. Lorraine came into some money when her grandfather died—oh, it must be twenty years ago or more. And she handled it well, made it last. But after she died—well, he just pissed it all away," he said heavily.

Alberg drew smoke coming from the engine, even though that didn't happen anymore.

"He'd talk about his people now and then," Quenneville went on, "his mom and dad, that is. Warmly. Good memories. But I only heard him mention that sister of his a couple of times, and it was plain as the nose on your face: he was scared of her."

Alberg paused in his sketching. "Why?"

"I don't know why, man—how would I know? But he sure was. Turned twitchy just saying her name. Never said it, unless he was boozing. Just a minute. Hold on." He talked with his wife. "Flora and I, we'll be bringing him home with us. She wants you to tell him that. The lawyer, he says it's in the will."

"I'll tell him, Mr. Quenneville."

"And see if you can get him on a phone to us."

"I will," said Alberg. His train now had an engine and eight cars.

Next, he called Edward Cherniak, Benjamin Strachan's lawyer, at the home number he'd gotten from Peter Quenneville.

He talked, and listened, and nodded, and added a caboose to his train, and listened some more, and drew a railway-crossing sign in front of the engine. "Did she say what would have been in this package?" he asked the lawyer.

"No," said Cherniak. "Just that it was something that was hers. She sounded angry that I didn't know where it might be."

Alberg asked a couple more questions, thanked the lawyer, and hung up.

His cats were demanding to be fed, so he got up and did that, and had breakfast himself, and showered and shaved. He was moving faster now. Beginning to feel excited. He noticed that fog clung to the hillside. He couldn't see the harbor; he could barely see the road in front of his house.

As soon as the banks opened, he sat down to make another phone call.

"Ms. Hawke? My name is Alberg. I'm with the RCMP in Sechelt. You're the manager, right? I need some information, and I wonder if you can help me. . . ."

A few minutes later he had arranged to meet Harriet Hawke at her bank in West Vancouver.

He peered once more out his front window and noticed, with relief, shimmerings of sunshine amid the fog.

He could be back at Zoe Strachan's house before dinner-time, he figured.

CHAPTER
42

There was a lawn chair set up in the yard behind her house, between the house and the sea, and there Ramona found herself about halfway through Wednesday morning, sitting tense and upright, clutching a big brown envelope. She turned to look behind her, at the house: what was she doing back at her old house? She looked in front of her, where the ocean should have been, but she couldn't see it because of the fog; she could only hear it. She knew it was morning, but she didn't know how she knew that, and she knew that she had something important to do, but she couldn't remember what.

She looked down at the brown envelope. She turned it over and over in her hands. The writing on it made no sense to her. Finally she opened it and peered inside and saw three exercise books and a note written in pencil on ruled paper. And then memory returned, and she almost wished it hadn't.

He hadn't told her not to read them, but let's face it, said Ramona to herself, shivering in the fog, it wouldn't have mattered if he had; she would have read them anyway. She wasn't about to accept a package from a scared-to-death little boy without looking inside it, and having identified the contents as reading material, she wasn't about to not read them.

So she'd read them. Right away, she'd read them. And afterward she got up from the kitchen table, where she'd been sitting as she read, and she felt sick with fear.

She tried to distract herself with a huge breakfast. She opened cans of flaked ham, sardines, oysters, and corned beef. She helped herself to Melba Toast and Wheat Thins and some Swedish flatbread. She drank some orange Australian stuff and ate an entire can of peaches. At the conclusion of her feast she'd felt bloated, dissatisfied, and more fearful and worried than ever. She finally admitted to herself that the police had to have these exercise books. And they had to be told about the boy. It took her a while to figure out how she was going to accomplish these things and hang on to her freedom, too.

Ramona struggled out of the lawn chair and made her way around to the front of the house. How much time had she lost? Too much? Too much? Had she come too late?

She held the brown envelope tight to her chest and tried to think. The fog hadn't lifted yet. So surely it had to be morning, still. Surely she hadn't missed him.

She squatted down and leaned against the fence and squinted into the fog and waited.

She waited for what seemed like a very long time. She stood up, now and then, to ease the cramp in her thighs. Sometimes she sat upon the ground with her legs stretched out straight in front of her, until she felt too damp and cold. She hummed to herself, and refused to accept the possibility that she might have missed Sandy McAllister. She just kept on waiting, grateful to the fog, which was keeping people indoors. And finally, finally, she heard him whistling, and just as he emerged out of the fog, she stepped into his path.

Sandy McAllister screamed.

"It's me," said Ramona. "Sandy, it's me, Ramona."

"The whole town," Sandy gasped, "is looking for you. The whole town, Ramona. The police. Everybody. Everybody is looking for you. Oh, I've found you. Oh. Oh."

"No, Sandy," said Ramona sternly. "You have not found me. I have found you." She held out the brown envelope. "You see this?" Sandy looked at it. "You see what it says on the front of it?"

" 'Head of Detachment, Sechelt RCMP,' " Sandy read aloud. "You look a sight, Ramona. You really do."

"I want you to deliver this," said Ramona. She thrust it at him, and Sandy backed away, clutching at his mailbag.

"I can't deliver it," he said. "You deliver it. Come on," he said excitedly. "I'll go with you. Come on, Ramona."

"I'm not going anywhere," said Ramona. "Take it," she said, poking him in the stomach with the brown envelope.

Sandy McAllister raised both hands in the air. "I won't," he said.

Ramona, furious, smacked him on the shoulder. "Take it! Deliver it! What kind of a mailman are you, anyway!"

"I can't, Ramona," he pleaded. "They're looking all over the place for you. They'll be some mad if I waltz in there with a package from you that's got no stamps on it. 'Where'd you get this?' they'll say to me. And what'll I tell them? I found it on the street or something? No, I'll say, 'Oh, Ramona gave it to me,' and they'll say, 'So where is she?' and then I'll say, 'Oh, she's in the bush next to the highway,' and then they'll say, 'So don't you know the whole town's looking for her?' and they'll

probably throw me in the slammer for obstruction of justice."
He stopped, breathless. "See?"

Ramona stared at him. She pretended to sigh. "Let me think
for a minute," she said.

Sandy McAllister watched, eagerly, as she thought.

Finally, "All right," she said. "I give up."

"Good," he said. He was beside himself with excitement.
"Oh, good, Ramona."

"But right now I'm too tired to move, Sandy," she said,
leaning upon him heavily. "You deliver this envelope to the
Mounties." She handed it to him, and this time he took it.
"Make sure it gets to the head man there, mind you. Then you
can tell them where I am. They can come and get me."

He looked at her, uncertain.

"I'll be fine, Sandy," she said. "I'll go on back into my house
there and wait for them."

He took a reluctant step away from her.

"Oh go on, go on," she said, exasperated, flapping her hand
at him.

Sandy McAllister backed away into the fog, and when she
was certain he was gone, Ramona hurried around the house
and headed up the beach for the promontory, and the cottage.

CHAPTER
43

Zoe, in the kitchen, turned to see the boy watching her from the hallway. She shook her head, thinking about Benjamin and his second wife going to such a lot of trouble to acquire this child. It's beyond me, she thought, looking at him, why on earth they wanted him.

"Come in here," she said, pleasantly enough. "I'm about to make your lunch."

She sat him down at the kitchen table, beneath the small square window that was set so high in the wall that he couldn't see anything through it without standing on a chair.

Zoe looked around the kitchen, frowning. "I can't remember what I'd planned to have." She would prepare the boy's meal and sit with him while he ate it. She preferred to eat alone and would wait until he was back in his room, watching television. "I think I was going to cook some pork chops," she said. "And scalloped potatoes."

She sat down at the table, opposite Kenny, and smoothed

her hand over its surface, first the right hand and then the left, in slow arcs; she did each hand five times. "It's important that I find those little books," she said.

Kenny didn't respond.

"I'm getting very tired of saying that to you."

He wiggled on his chair. "I told you. I don't know where they are."

She told herself that it was important to think things out slowly and carefully, in order to forestall the emotional turmoil in which anger might flourish.

"Where were you going this morning?" she asked him.

"I told you. I wasn't going anywhere. I was just walking around. Exploring."

"Exploring? In the fog?"

He shrugged.

"It was extremely thoughtless of you to leave the house without asking. I was very worried about you."

He kicked at the table leg, not hard but stubbornly. She didn't like his attitude.

"I'm responsible for you right now," she said. "You could have fallen on the rocks. Or into the sea."

"I was just looking around."

She arched her spine and rubbed at the small of her back with her fists. They were probably in the safe-deposit box in his damn bank, she thought. But they might be in the house. They could still be in the house. She might have missed them. It was certainly true that the boy popping up like that had rattled her. "He had hiding places when he was a boy," she said. She laughed. "All over the house, he had them."

"But how do you know that he even had them? If they're yours, why would Dad have them?"

She smiled. "I know he had them," she said softly, "because

227

I saw it in your face." He started to protest; she clicked her tongue and shook her finger at him. "Don't argue. I know what I saw. But you're right about one thing. He *shouldn't* have had them. He most certainly should not have had them." She leaned across the table. "He stole them. That's how he got them."

"My dad wouldn't steal. You can't say things like that." His face was red and angry, even though Zoe could tell that he was still afraid of her.

She looked at him impassively. She sat back. "Maybe you're right. Maybe he just found them somewhere. In an old trunk or something. Anyway, it doesn't matter. He was going to give them back to me. That's the important thing. And it isn't fair that I shouldn't be able to get them, just because he died before he could give them to me."

"How do you know he was going to give them to you?" There was a perpetual whine in the boy's voice that grated badly on Zoe's nerves.

"Because he said so," she snapped.

Kenny looked uncertain.

"When he came to my house," she said. "That's *why* he came to my house."

"How come he didn't bring them with him, then?"

"Oh, for heaven's sake." She stood up and went over to the refrigerator, wrenched open the door and got a package of pork chops from the freezer. She tossed them onto the counter next to the microwave oven. She went back to the table and squatted down next to him. "Your business is to help me find my scribblers. They're somewhere in that house. Your business is to help me find them."

"I don't know where they are," he said. "I really don't."

She gazed at him, "I have a long-standing aversion," she

said, "to children. That means that I don't like them."

"I could—"

"Yes yes. I know. You could go stay with Roddy." She stood up and got potatoes from a drawer in the fridge. "Not yet."

"When are we going to have my dad's funeral?"

"Ask that policeman, next time you see him."

After a while she put down the potato she was peeling and sat again at the table. "You know," she said thoughtfully, "I don't think I've told you what's in those little books."

"I don't care," said Kenny. "It's all right."

"They're books I wrote things in when I was a child."

"You don't have to tell me anything."

"I called them my scribblers. That's what they were. Scribblers. Exercise books."

The boy became silent.

"I wrote stories in them. You know? Do you understand? Made-up stories. Like stories you read in books."

He stared at the floor and didn't speak.

"Not true things, you idiot child. Pretend things. Made-up things. Do you understand?" She realized she was shouting at him. He looked tense and brittle, and he didn't speak.

CHAPTER
44

By late afternoon, as Alberg was returning once more to the house on the promontory, the whole town knew that Ramona Orlitzki had been found.

And lost again.

Alberg had spoken to Isabella by phone from West Vancouver and with Sid Sokolowski on the radio as he drove up from the ferry at Langdale. He hoped Sandy McAllister had enjoyed his ten minutes of glory, because he was now in complete disgrace. Isabella wasn't speaking to him anymore, and Sid wanted to charge him with something. Sid was enraged. And Alberg sympathized. It was damned embarrassing, the whole detachment outwitted by a seventy-five-year-old woman whose mind wasn't supposed to be working right.

At least they knew she was still alive, he thought, pulling into Zoe Strachan's driveway. And apparently well. At least her idiot son Horace knew she was alive; that, thought

Alberg, was very satisfying indeed. He hoped the PI had charged old Horace an arm and a leg.

He climbed out of his car and advanced wearily upon Zoe Strachan's house. He knew very little more than he'd known that morning. He had no reason, really, to come here—except that he'd promised Kenny.

He knocked on the door, and she opened it and smiled, as though she'd been expecting him.

In the living room the sun slanted low through the French doors, laying great swaths of light upon the carpet, glittering in Zoe Strachan's black hair.

"Has it been decided yet," she said, stroking the arm of the leather chair in which she sat, "whether an inquest will be held?"

"Let me ask you something first," said Alberg, from the sofa. "Why were you trying to get into your brother's safe-deposit box?"

She studied him for a long time. He thought again of a searchlight, but this time he knew himself to be inscrutable. He gazed back at her placidly, and saw in his mind Kenny's face imprisoned between the slats of the venetian blind.

"His will," she said at last. "I wanted to know what was to be done with the boy." She shifted position, arched her back slightly. "How did you know?"

Alberg grinned at her.

"She let *you* into his safe-deposit box?"

He shrugged, careless.

"Gestapo," she said, absentmindedly, still staring at him.

"It's my understanding," said Alberg, "that Kenny's to go to his grandparents."

"Yes," said Zoe. "I talked to the lawyer."

"So did I," said Alberg.

"Did you," said Zoe.

Alberg felt suddenly weightless, as though the air had thinned drastically.

"You haven't answered my question," she said. "About the inquest."

Alberg hesitated. Then "No," he said. "I don't think there'll be an inquest."

She remained impassive, but Alberg experienced a disengagement of something. He realized that Zoe had let go. For a moment he felt lost; abandoned.

"I expect you'd like to see the boy," she said, and stood up, effortlessly, in a single movement, like an athlete. "I'll get him."

He watched her go, and felt an unaccountable sadness.

Kenny curled quickly up on the bed when he heard her coming down the hall. She opened the door without knocking, the way she always did. She was looking very cold in her face. "The policeman's here," she said. He already knew that; he'd heard the doorbell ring and had peeked out into the hall and seen him.

He followed her to the living room.

"I phoned Roddy," said the policeman, smiling at him.

Kenny sat on the edge of the wing chair.

"Well, I phoned his parents," Alberg amended. "I talked to his mom. She's very sorry about your dad, Kenny."

"Did they say I could stay with them?" He had to clear his throat in the middle of the sentence; it was so dry the words just barely squeaked out.

"You don't need to stay with them," said Zoe. "You're staying with me. You can't stay in two places at once, now can you?"

Kenny and the policeman looked at her, then at each other.

"We'll see," said Alberg. "Your aunt and I will talk about it."

Kenny felt a little better.

"I called your grandparents, too," said Alberg. "They'll be here on Saturday."

"Wonderful," said Zoe, and sat down in her leather chair.

"They liked your brother," the policeman said to her. "And they're very fond of Kenny."

"Yeah," said Kenny. He rubbed at his right eye with the back of his hand.

"They want you to live with them from now on," said Alberg.

Kenny felt his eyes fill suddenly with tears.

"It's what your dad wanted, too," said Alberg.

Kenny slid out of his chair and went to sit next to the policeman on the sofa. "I wanted to go with him," he said. "I asked my dad to take me with him. But he wouldn't." He looked quickly over at Zoe, then down at his hands.

"I guess he didn't want you to miss school," said Alberg.

Kenny leaned closer. "He didn't want anything bad to happen to me, ever," he said, so softly that Alberg almost couldn't hear.

Across the room, his aunt stirred in her chair. "When did you say his grandparents are arriving, Staff Sergeant?" she said. She got up and came over to Kenny and rested her fingers in his hair. It felt as if some flying bugs had landed there, on his head.

"Saturday," said the policeman, looking at Kenny. "I've got an idea. They'd like to talk to Kenny, Miss Strachan. Why don't I take him to a phone and let him give them a call?"

Kenny could tell she was looking down at him, right at the top of his head.

"When do they leave?" she said.

"Tomorrow. Noon," said Alberg.

She lifted her hand from Kenny's head, stepped back, and folded her arms. She put a playful look on her face. "I don't see why not," she said, and for a minute there was a big surge of happiness in Kenny's chest, and then she said, "I'll tell you what. Come for him early in the morning. Take him out for breakfast, if you like."

"Is that okay, Kenny?" said the policeman, looking carefully at his face, into his eyes. Maybe he'd be able to see for himself that it wasn't okay, thought Kenny.

"Sure," he said.

The policeman gave him a one-armed hug around the shoulders. "Seven o'clock, then. Okay?"

"Okay," said Kenny. And maybe it would be.

C H A P T E R

45

When Sandy McAllister scampered into the detachment Wednesday morning, he dumped the mail on the counter, and blurted out the news about Ramona, and girded himself for herohood.

It was much later in the day that Isabella, tired and distraught, scooped the mail from the counter onto her desk and sorted it. The brown envelope addressed to the head of the detachment had "PERSONAL" written on it in big letters, so she took it into Alberg's office and placed it, unopened, on his desk.

Alberg found it there in the evening, when he stopped in on his way home from Zoe Strachan's house.

There was no return address on the envelope. He opened it cautiously, but found inside only three dog-eared exercise books and a note. "Please read these," said the note, which was written in pencil, on ruled paper, "and look after the boy at the Strachan woman's house." "Please" was underlined twice.

Alberg looked again at the envelope. He opened one of the exercise books and felt a lurch in his stomach: "PRIVATE PROPERTY OF ZOE STRACHAN. DO NOT READ. ON PAIN OF DEATH." He called Isabella at home.

"Where did it come from?" he asked.

"It came in the mail," said Isabella.

"I don't think so," said Alberg. "There's no stamp on it. No postmark."

"I'm sure of it," said Isabella. "It was in the mail."

"Okay," said Alberg, thumbing through the yellow scribbler. He hung up and found Sandy McAllister's number in the directory. But Sandy either wasn't in or had decided not to answer his phone.

Alberg began to read.

A half hour later, he put the exercise books and the note back into the envelope. With the side of his hand he pushed the envelope to the edge of his desk. He sat quietly, looking at the envelope, but his hands were pressed hard against the surface of the desk in front of him, as if he might suddenly push himself upright.

Eventually he reached for the phone and made three calls. The last was to Sid Sokolowski. When the sergeant arrived, Alberg thrust the yellow exercise book at him and told him to read.

Sokolowski read.

"Shit," said the sergeant, dazed. He looked up from the pages, covered in childish handwriting. "Is it true, or what?"

"I'm getting it checked out. But I think it is, yeah."

"Then we'd be talking about an indictable offense."

Alberg nodded.

"How old do you figure she was?"

"I've read all three of those goddamn books. She was twelve."

"Jesus," said the sergeant. He placed the yellow scribbler carefully back into the envelope. "Could we get a conviction?"

"Probably," said Alberg. "If it's true. I called the Justice. He's on his way."

"We're gonna need two warrants."

"Yeah," said Alberg. "I told him."

"How do you want to handle it?"

"The most important thing . . ." He got up and went to the window. He pulled the blind all the way up, then let it fall. "I want to get that kid out of there. We can't Charter and warn her until we get a lab report on the handwriting. That won't be until at least sometime tomorrow. I'm not waiting. We've got to get him out of there now."

"Yeah," said Sokolowski. "I'll call Frieda, tell her to come down here." Frieda Listad worked for the provincial ministry of social services. She was also another of Sid Sokolowski's wife's cousins: a sister to Ludmilla.

"I was hoping you'd say that," said Alberg, with relief.

"Sure. There's reasonable and probable grounds, Karl. To worry about the kid. That's all she needs."

There was a tap on the door. The duty officer leaned in. "The Justice is here, Staff."

"I'll be right out," said Alberg. "Okay," he said to Sokolowski. "Ask Frieda to get over here fast. As soon as we get it confirmed that this—this incident actually happened, we'll move. I want Frieda to go with us. We'll serve the warrants, get the samples, and Frieda can apprehend the boy."

"Karl," said Sokolowski, reaching for the phone. "How'd you get hold of those exercise books, anyway?"

"Not sure," said Alberg, shrugging into his jacket. "I think maybe from Ramona."

The sergeant's mouth fell open. "Oh, hey, Ramona?" he protested, incredulous. "Ramona?"

"Ramona," said Alberg. "Via Sandy McAllister."

CHAPTER

46

She was filled with anger again, after all this time. She was afraid to look in a mirror again, after all this time: afraid she would see that her eyes were bulging, pushed from her head by the fury that was jammed in there. She felt like a child again, helpless in the grip of rage.

She struggled with it for a long time.

Then she looked around for the boy, but he'd disappeared.

He's gone, she thought, and flew down the hall. She threw open the door to his room and flicked on the overhead light. He was in his pajamas, in bed; maybe he'd been asleep.

"I have to think," she said aloud, and pressed the heels of her hands against her temples.

She went downstairs to her workroom, turned on the light, and shut herself inside. She brushed paint remover on the surface of the sideboard and sat back to wait.

She tapped her feet on the cement floor, first one, then the other.

She heard the clicking of her leather soles on the floor, and, bewildered, she lifted her arms and stared down at herself. Why was she not wearing her worn sneakers? Why was she still wearing the good wool slacks and the white silk shirt she'd put on in the morning? Why hadn't she changed into her old jeans and a baggy old sweatshirt and an old pair of sneakers before coming down here?

She had to lean over awkwardly now, while she worked, so as to keep her clothes clean.

Carefully she maneuvered the scraper across the wood, scraping up a long strip of puckered brown paint; but she hadn't let it sit long enough, and paint still clung stubbornly to the wood. She scraped harder and faster, and suddenly the scraper slipped and struck the side of her hand, which began to bleed.

Zoe grabbed a roll of paper towels from a shelf and pressed some against her hand. But blood had already spattered her slacks and her silk shirt.

Wearily, she looked around her workroom. The sideboard was the last piece left to do. The walls were lined with pieces of furniture she had meticulously refinished. There were rows and rows of them. It was time to empty the place again. She would rent a truck, as soon as this business with the wretched boy was out of the way, and take the finished pieces out to the dump. Then she would set about assembling another batch, from antique- and used-furniture shops up and down the Coast and on the Lower Mainland.

Her hand was throbbing. Cautiously, she peeked under the wadded-up paper toweling. The bleeding seemed to be slowing down. She turned off the light and climbed the stairs, aching and disconsolate.

But at least the anger had gone.

In the bathroom that adjoined her bedroom she cleaned her injured hand and bandaged it. She took off her slacks and shirt and stuffed them into the wastebasket in her bedroom. She put on jeans, sweatshirt, and sneakers, ran a comb through her hair, took two aspirin, and went down the hall to the boy's room.

She opened the door and told him to come to the living room.

"Until today," she said to him, when they were sitting down, she in her leather chair, he, wearing his pajamas, in the chair by the doorway, "I had thought you might not know where my scribblers are. But today I know that you do."

She felt her heartbeat quicken and turned slightly, so she could look away from the boy. She must not permit herself to become angry again. And it was this proximity to the child that was doing it. Her brain became distressed and heedless in the presence of this child.

He sat there looking thin and anxious, and then he began to cry.

"We're going to the house," she said. "You and I."

"The house?" His voice was scratchy. He cleared his throat. "My house?"

"And you're going to help me find my scribblers."

"But—but you already looked there. You already looked in my house."

"They cannot be anywhere else," said Zoe. "They were not in his pockets, they were not in his car," she said, ticking off on her fingers, "and the policeman as much as told me they are not in his safe-deposit box. Therefore they have to be in his office or in the house." She looked vaguely around her. "I'm quite sure they're not in his office. Therefore they must be in the house."

"I don't know where they are. It's true. It's true."

Zoe stood up and clasped her hands tightly together. "Really, this weeping, it isn't advisable. I don't think you fully comprehend your situation. Really."

He sniveled and snorted, and swiped at his nose with the back of his hand. He was a weak, scraggly, scrawny piece of humanity, every bit as useless as his father.

"You'd better get your jacket," she said coldly, and watched as he slithered reluctantly down the hall.

She went to the closet for her raincoat, and returned to the living room. She sat down and switched on the television, flipping from channel to channel. She couldn't understand what anybody was saying. It was as though they were speaking in various incomprehensible languages.

Finally, growing impatient, she looked at her watch. With a shock, she saw that it was midnight. She had missed the last ferry.

Slowly, her eyes blank, Zoe stood up. Tremors rippled through her shoulder muscles. Her hands were clenched into fists. She battled savagely to control herself . . . and she might have won, she might have prevailed, if she hadn't gone down the hall to tell the boy he could go back to sleep; if she hadn't opened his door, and seen his empty bed, and the open window.

CHAPTER
47

That night, fog had again crept in from the sea, and down from the hilltops.

It enveloped Zoe Strachan's house, and the cottage where Ramona Orlitzki watched television and sipped her gin and wondered whether the police had rescued the boy yet.

Cassandra Mitchell looked from her kitchen window and couldn't see ocean, or the Indian graveyard, or even the highway that passed fifty yards from her front door. But she saw lights, blurred and distant, and for a moment imagined that she was in a ship, gazing through fog at the lights of an unfamiliar country.

Karl Alberg got restless, waiting for the phone to ring, and decided to pace around the block a couple of times. He walked outside unprepared for fog and there it was, damp fingers in his hair, a moist palm pressed lightly against his face. He changed his mind about going for a walk. He wondered if the fog would be even thicker, denser, when it was time to go back to Zoe Strachan's house. It wasn't that he minded it, he told himself. It just made driving unpleasant. He hated it when the fog was so thick that his headlights made yellow dents in it but couldn't cut through it. He hated it when he rolled down his window and stuck his head out, to see better, and felt the oily caress of the fog against his face, and imagined it slithering into his lungs; he tried not to breathe then. He found he wasn't breathing now, standing outside the detachment. So he went indoors again.

Just after midnight, Zoe Strachan closed and locked Kenny's window. Then she tied her raincoat tight around her and emerged from her house into the fog, brandishing a flashlight.

Ramona thought she heard somebody tapping at the door. At first she ignored it, trying not to be frightened. Then she got up and opened the door, and the boy was there, and she let him in, and the fog swirled around the cottage and drifted among the branches of the fir trees.

CHAPTER
48

The fog surged around her, and Zoe imagined the boy hiding in it, peeking around it and through it; seeing her when she couldn't see him. It hurt her eyes because it wouldn't hold still; it fluttered and throbbed, advanced and retreated, and sometimes she had to close her eyes against it—but not for long; she was too close to the rocks, to the sea.

She circled her house, shining the flashlight beam across the patio, bending over to try to focus it down into the nooks and crannies of the rocky beach, but there was only whiteness down there, sometimes impenetrable, sometimes wispy, with black water moving restlessly behind it. The cold ocean breezes were pushing more and more fog onto the land, piling it up, like stricken clouds, upon her property. How would she explain it if the boy ended up dead, broken on the rocks or drowned in the Pacific? She wouldn't need to explain it, she told herself. If the child is stupid enough to wander outside in the middle of the night, in the middle of a bank of fog, then he deserves to smash himself against the rocks, or perish in the sea.

She didn't want to find him dead. She wanted to find him alive. It was just possible . . . if she could get hold of him before he found his way to the damned policeman or a damned pay phone, she would drive them straight to Langdale, and they'd wait in the car for the six o'clock ferry. . . .

If she could just get the damned scribblers.

She was shaking with rage. She stopped, rested, took several deep breaths, tried desperately to relax . . . but the thought of that wretched child was enough to send her blood pressure skyrocketing.

Stop it, Zoe, she said. Stop it.

Think.

She'd circled the house, checked the beach, as much as that was possible. She had heard no whimperings, no whinings, no sounds except sea sounds, wind sounds, and her own labored breathing.

Surely he would have fled along the driveway, she thought. Not in the middle of it but to one side.

He'd be running, not walking, and he had a head start. And Zoe, rational again, got into her car and began driving toward the highway.

The headlights caused the fog to dance and flutter. Zoe was peering intently out the window, and driving very slowly, but she couldn't see anything, because of the fog, and the glare of the headlights. She switched the lights off; the car crunched blindly down the driveway but she was going so slowly she wasn't worried about accidents, collisions; she'd driven along here so often she knew exactly where she was, even in the fog. When she got to the highway she'd turn the headlights back on and drive toward Sechelt.

But what if he was already there, at the police station, or calling his damned friend Roddy? But he couldn't be there yet, she thought, he hadn't had time to get to Sechelt yet—and then off to the left she saw a wink of light, right where the cottage ought to be.

The cottage. The cottage. That damned brat is in my cottage.

49

"Shit," said Alberg, banging down the phone.

"No luck?" said Sokolowski.

"No luck. Jesus. You'd think with all the computers in the world . . ."

"Oh, well, computers," said the sergeant, with contempt.

"I don't want to wait any longer, Sid."

"Well, yeah, I know what you mean. We got the warrants. Frieda's sitting out there, ready to go. But, Karl, kids make things up. If it turns out she made it all up . . ."

Alberg's phone rang, and he grabbed it eagerly, but it turned out to be Cassandra.

"I tried your house," she said. "You're working awfully late, aren't you?"

"Yeah, I am. Cassandra, listen—"

Sokolowski lumbered to his feet. "You talk to her, Karl. Relax for a minute."

"You're busy," said Cassandra. "I won't keep you."

Sokolowski gave Alberg a reassuring nod. "Five minutes," he said. "Give them another five minutes." He backed out of Alberg's office, closing the door behind him.

"I've got five minutes," said Alberg into the phone. "How are you? How's your mom?"

"Fine. We're both fine. I wanted to say, why don't you stop by for coffee, or a drink, on your way home?"

"I'm going to be pretty late, Cassandra."

"That's okay. Really." She sounded wistful. Subdued.

"If I can," said Alberg softly.

"What's going on down there anyway? How come you're still at work?"

"I'll tell you after."

"After what?"

"After it's all over."

Sokolowski knocked, and stuck his head in. "We got it, Karl."

"I've gotta go, Cassandra." He said goodbye and hung up. "Did they call?" he said to Sokolowski.

"Yeah. It happened, Karl. Just like she wrote it down."

A siren sounded, starting small, building loud and clamorous, summoning members of the volunteer fire department.

Alberg went to the window and pulled up the blind. "I can't see a thing in this damn fog."

They hurried down the hall to the reception area, where Frieda Listad waited. The duty officer was just hanging up the phone. "Staff?" he said. "The fire. It's down at the Strachan place."

Alberg and Sokolowski stared at one another.

"Let's go, Sid," said Alberg quietly.

C H A P T E R

50

The cottage had two doors. The back door led directly into the kitchen. There was a tiny hall closet between the front door and the bedroom. When Ramona let the boy in, he was so frightened that to soothe him she barricaded both the doors. With his help she wrestled a tall chest of drawers from the bedroom into the hall and wedged it up against the front door. There wasn't much they could do in the kitchen except put the table in the way of the door, so that's what they did.

The boy said his name was Kenny.

She forgot at first that she knew him.

"What did you do with them?" he said urgently, looking around the cottage, once they'd done the barricading.

"With what?" she said.

"It—with the thing I gave you. You know. The brown envelope."

She gazed at him, uncomprehending.

"I gave it to you," he said, beginning to cry. "This morning."

"Are you sure it was me?" she said, feeling panicky.

"I gave it to you. In the fog," said Kenny, sobbing. "I did."

"Oh my goodness," she said. "Oh yes. I'm sorry. I remember now." She gave him a hug. "Don't you worry, they're in good hands. I got them delivered straight to the police."

"I—you mean you opened it up? You read them?"

"Of course I did," said Ramona. She leaned close to him. "I don't blame you one bit for being scared. I was scared, too, reading that stuff."

"What'll happen now?" said Kenny.

"First I'm going to make you something hot to eat," said Ramona. She got one of the fancy packages of chicken noodle soup down from the cupboard. "Too bad I don't have any milk. I'll have to make it with water."

"And then what?" said the boy, and Ramona told him that just as soon as it was light enough, she would take him out of the cottage and down the driveway and along the beach to the first of the houses there, and they would call the police and tell them where to come and get him.

After he'd eaten, they sat on the bed and watched late-night TV.

"Did you hear something?" he said, for the third time since he'd gotten there.

Dutifully, Ramona turned the sound down on the television and listened. "No."

"I thought I heard something."

"I don't think so." She smoothed some hair away from his forehead. It was like having her own children back—she'd always liked Horace and Martha, when they were children.

Ramona turned the sound back up. "Just as soon as it's light, we'll skedaddle on out of here."

"Yeah. Good."

"Can you bring me some fruit, do you think?"

"You mean, afterwards?" said Kenny.

"Yes. Before you go home."

"Yeah. Sure. Sure I will. You're gonna stay here, then, right?"

"For a little while longer, anyway. Until the people come back."

He looked at her quizzically, and was about to say something, but changed his mind.

A commercial break interrupted the movie, and Ramona, chuckling with pleasure, triumphantly used the remote control device to turn off the sound.

"Shhh!" said the boy. "I heard something," he whispered. He shuffled himself over closer to Ramona, who put her bony arm around his shoulder and strained to hear whatever he had heard.

Suddenly a great pounding began. It took Ramona a minute to figure out that it was coming from the front door.

"It's her!" said the boy, and he shot out of bed, looking around him wildly.

The noise was thunderous, implacable.

"My lord," said Ramona, thrusting her bare feet into slippers. She grabbed the boy and hustled him into the kitchen.

The hammering stopped, they heard quick footsteps at the side of the house, and it started again, this time at the back door, bang! bang! bang! rhythmic and horrifying.

"Who are you! What do you want!" Ramona shouted. She pushed the boy behind her.

"Get out of my house!" bellowed a female voice.

Ramona shook her head and leaned against the fridge. She

was intensely agitated. She couldn't remember what she'd done with the remote control device. She kept clicking it and clicking it, but there was nothing in her hand: she could see that it was empty.

"What are we gonna do!" cried the boy.

Ramona turned around to stare at him. The pounding on the kitchen door continued. It was apparently real sound—the door was shuddering on its hinges. . . .

Ramona said calmly to the boy, "She's going to get tired of banging like that. She's just doing it to scare us. Pretty soon she's going to break that window there, that kitchen window, or maybe the one in the living room, and climb right in here."

She hurried into the living room and picked up the poker from beside the Franklin stove. "Turn off that lamp in the bedroom. Turn off the TV, too," she said to him. "Go on! Do it!" And he did.

Ramona crouched by the kitchen window, just beside it, and sure enough, the banging on the door stopped. For a moment nothing happened. "Please God please God," said Ramona, over and over again, and then the window glass crashed into the kitchen. Ramona screamed and shut her eyes as the glass showered around and upon her. Then she lashed out with the poker, and heard a shriek of pain.

The woman went away then. The boy said, "She's gonna come back! Let's get out of here, let's get out of here!" Ramona didn't want to move. Her heart was all panicky and no wonder either, and her legs were too shaky to stand on. She told him to go without her, to pull out the pieces of broken glass and climb out the window and run and run and run, but he said he wasn't going without her. He was crying a lot, and Ramona felt very sorry for him.

"Oh please, please," he said, "let's go, please!"

Ramona was dizzy, and she hurt in a lot of places, she couldn't figure out just where, or why; she thought she could smell gasoline; she could see some blood, and realized that she must have fallen down in the broken glass, or maybe been hit by it when it fell into the house; but the worst thing was the hurricane that was going on inside her. It was a hurricane of confusion, of profound disorder; it bordered on anarchy, maybe even derangement: she wanted to know where Anton was when she needed him, and how Horace had ever grown up to be such an unpleasant person, and why she had ever agreed to that third operation—she oughtn't ever to have done that; it was the third operation that had caused all her troubles, she knew it. . . .

Ramona became aware of smoke, and heat, and the boy screaming.

"Where the hell have I gotten myself to?" she said. "Where on earth did this fire come from?"

She struggled to her feet and tottered into the bedroom. She flung open the cedar chest and hauled out a blanket.

The boy was screaming louder, and there were flames in the cottage as well as smoke, and the noise of fire was deafening. Ramona thought about the chicken noodle soup she'd made, and she couldn't remember if she'd turned off the stove; and she began to sob.

She dragged the blanket into the bathroom. "Here, come in here with me," she called, and Kenny ran after her.

"What are we gonna do! We're gonna burn to death!" he said.

"No," said Ramona, "no." She turned on the water taps full blast and dumped the blanket into the tub. "Wait," she said, grabbing at his sleeve. "Don't go out there."

"The window's too small!" he yelled, staring up at the bathroom window.

"Yes, yes," said Ramona.

She dragged the blanket from the tub and wrapped it around him. She pushed him out of the bathroom and through the cottage. Her eyes and throat stung from the smoke. She heard the fire crackling and thought about fat melting, flesh melting; she felt the fire on her skin, but it didn't hurt.

"Go!" she said, and shoved the boy through the flames, through the broken kitchen window. She was going to go back and get another blanket but it was too hot, too smoky. I wonder if I'm going to get rescued? she thought, sinking onto the kitchen floor.

CHAPTER

51

People ran up from the houses along the beach to watch, to help if they could. The first of them to arrive saw Kenny stumbling along the driveway, half caught in a sodden blanket, his hair singed, his face smudged with smoke. The man from the house down the beach caught the boy in his arms and said, "It's all right, you're safe now. The fire engines are coming—can you hear them?"

Kenny gestured frantically at the burning cottage. "She's still in there!" he said, and then the fire engine arrived and the man told the firefighters, "This boy was in the fire. I'm taking him to my place. But he says there's somebody else in there; a woman."

"Is it Miss Strachan?" the fireman asked Kenny.

"No no, it's an old lady, an old lady!" said the boy, and the fireman said they'd try to get her out, and the man, a big strong man with gray hair, carried Kenny off along the driveway and down to the beach and over the sand to the house where he lived with his wife.

The cottage fell in on itself, all fire and noise, and nobody could go in there to get the old lady out.

Alberg arrived, with Frieda Listad and Sid Sokolowski. The firefighters were shouting at one another as they hosed down the fir trees surrounding the burning building. Alberg asked one of them if anyone had been inside.

And the firefighter replied, "Yeah. A kid. Said his name's Kenny. He's okay. Brian Forbes took him to his place. The kid said there was a woman, too." He shook his head. He was smoke-smeared, already exhausted. "But there was nothing we could do."

"I'll see to the boy," said Frieda Listad. "I know where Brian Forbes lives."

"Good," said Sid Sokolowski. "Give us a call later, okay?"

When she'd gone, Alberg said, "It's Ramona." He was staring at the fire. "Ramona's in there." He glanced across the circle of spectators and saw Zoe Strachan standing motionless, apart from the others. "Come on," he said to Sokolowski. He started walking toward her. She saw him and turned away, heading for the house.

They followed her. Zoe Strachan walked not slowly, not quickly, and they kept pace behind her, three pairs of feet scrunching on the gravel. Alberg, uneasy in the fog, was anxious not to lose sight of her, yet it seemed he couldn't hurry. It was a dreamlike experience, following her up the gravel driveway as if he'd been summoned. The shouts of the firefighters grew fainter. The fog seemed to grow thicker. The sea talked to the night, to the fog, in a restless, broody mutter. Alberg walked, and Sid trailed quietly in his wake, and Alberg watched Zoe Strachan's arms swinging, her hips swaying, and he remembered having had all those lustful thoughts about her, and he realized that he had them still.

As they approached her house he saw her car parked askew in the driveway, the driver's door open. She reached the doorstep and turned to face them.

"I have here two warrants," said Alberg.

Zoe looked behind him, at Sid Sokolowski. She seemed very calm.

"One of them," said Alberg, "permits me to retain possession of three exercise books apparently belonging to you, which were delivered anonymously to the Sechelt detachment, RCMP—"

Zoe Strachan smiled, very faintly.

"The other," said Alberg, "is a warrant to seize known samples of your handwriting."

"Such a lot of fuss," said Zoe Strachan. "What was the age," she said carefully, "of the person who wrote in those scribblers?"

"Twelve," said Alberg.

"Twelve," said Zoe. She shook her head. "That's very young."

"Yeah," said Alberg. "But old enough to know what she was doing. And old enough to be charged for it." He leaned slightly closer to her. "Have you been at it again, Ms. Strachan?"

There was no response.

"I think you have."

He heard through the drifting fog only the sound of the sea.

"We need the samples, now," he said, holding out the warrant.

She looked at it for a moment. Then she raised her eyes to Alberg's face and gave him a smile of such warmth and charm that he was sure she must have misunderstood him. "Of course," she said. "I'll be happy to cooperate."

CHAPTER
52

The fog was poking and prodding around the house, so as soon as the policemen left, Zoe locked all the doors and windows and turned the heat up high.

It was such a relief, having her house all to herself again.

Her shoulder was very sore, where it had been struck, so she ran a hot bath, poured in several handfuls of Yardley's bath salts, undressed, and soaked for almost an hour, sipping white wine. She added more hot water whenever she began cooling off.

Eventually the pain in her shoulder dulled, and she felt herself relaxing. She closed her eyes, enjoying the fragrance of the bath salts, running her hands slowly across her body, feeling sleepy and voluptuous.

All a person needed, she thought, to ensure her physical and mental health, was solitude; seclusion.

* * *

The rage was big and strong and getting all the time bigger and stronger. Zoe imagined anger taking up all the room in her body, growing and growing, pushing other stuff out. Her eyes would pop out of their sockets, her brain would squeeze itself out through her mouth, all the yucky things inside her, intestines and stuff, would push out where she had BMs. It was very scary.

She didn't even need the old people's trees anymore, because she'd found an even better private outdoor place. But that didn't make any difference to the size of her anger.

She found it down the road, past where the gravel began. She was going along the road one day, the dust from the gravel getting all over her feet in their brown sandals, turning her sandals gray just like her feet, and next to the road was a field that didn't have anything in it except weeds. Beyond the field were some trees—not a whole bunch of them like a forest, just a few. She ran across the field and through the trees, looking carefully around for signs of people or wild animals, but she didn't see anything. On the other side of the trees the land kind of dipped, and at the bottom of the dip was a big old barn. This became her private outdoor place.

The front door of the barn was broken and hanging open. The first time she went inside she heard some rustling, and her skin got all cold and crawly; then she saw a cat looking at her from behind a big piece of rusty machinery. Zoe moved a little bit away from the door, and the cat ran to it and through it and far away.

At the side of the barn was a ladder. She climbed it and found a bunch of hay up there, and a kind of window, without any glass in it. She liked to lie down in the hay and look over the edge to the big floor of the barn down below her. There was always a lot of dust, and when the sun shone the air was full of little bits of floating stuff.

It smelled good in the barn. And maybe she was the only person in the world who knew it was there.

She started going there almost every day, except when it rained, because then it was chilly and clammy in the hay. She was very glad she'd found it; it was much better than sitting up in a dumb apple tree.

But she was still jam-packed with rage. She found things in the barn, tools made of metal all rough and flaky with rust, and she banged with them at the dirt floor and the hanging-down door, using all her strength, and this made her tired, but she was still just as angry as ever.

One day when she'd done this she climbed up the ladder and lay down on the hay, and then all of a sudden there was a picture in her head, Zoe climbing the side fence into the old people's yard and nobody seeing her because it was night.

She wondered why she hadn't thought of this before.

Zoe began to feel drowsy in the bath; it was difficult to keep her eyes open, and her limbs felt flimsy, unsubstantial.

She pulled the plug, set her wineglass on the floor, and got on her knees to wash her hair under the tap.

When she was out of the tub and wrapped in a terry-cloth robe, she cleaned and dried the entire bathroom thoroughly.

Then she used the hair dryer. Her hair was thick and glossy, and she had never minded the silver in it.

It was very quiet in her bedroom when she turned off the dryer.

Suddenly she was stricken by melancholy. She sat on the edge of her bed and doubted, for a few moments, the wisdom of every decision she had ever made.

That night she didn't go to sleep when she went to bed. She kept herself awake by planning. It seemed a very long time, though, before the rest of the people in her house were asleep. She kept on just about dozing off. Finally she got up and moved her desk chair underneath one of the windows, and opened the window. Then she sat in the chair wearing only her nightgown, and the cool air coming in the window made her shiver and kept her awake.

Late at night she heard her parents come upstairs. She heard their voices for a while, although she couldn't tell what they were saying; then she heard their bedroom door close, and everything was quiet.

She knew that Benjamin wasn't in bed yet. He probably wasn't even home yet, from wherever he'd gone with his friends. Zoe was starting to get cold, and she was impatient, too. Either she had to go right away or she'd have to wait for Benjamin, and she didn't know how long he'd be, he might be hours, and even when he got home he might not go right to sleep. After thinking about it for a few minutes she put on her bathrobe and her slippers, opened her bedroom door very carefully, listened but heard nothing, and made her way slowly, on tiptoe, down the stairs.

Without turning on any lights, she found the big bowl full of books of matches that her mother kept in the kitchen. In the living room she emptied the basket that held wood for the fireplace and put back into it a few little pieces and two big ones and the newspaper that was lying on the coffee table.

She hurried across the lawn, the basket hitting against the side of her leg, and climbed awkwardly over the fence. She squatted down and waited for a minute, almost expecting to hear her mother yelling from an upstairs window, or the old people pushing open their squeaky screen door; but she didn't hear anything at all except a little bit of wind pushing through the vegetable garden in front of her.

She got up on her knees and looked over the vegetables to the old people's house. It was dark and quiet. Zoe's heart was hammering away in her chest. After a while she got up and began to sneak toward the house. The grass was damp, and so were the bottoms of her slippers. Her bathrobe got caught on a rosebush for a minute; she had to put down the basket and use both hands to pull herself free.

When she was near the house she squatted down again and listened some more, but still she heard nothing, and no light came on.

She scooted underneath the back porch and waited for a minute, listening as hard as she could, before getting out the newspaper, to be really sure nobody was awake in that house.

Then she made a fire.

After a while Zoe rallied.

She went to her closet and thought about what to wear.

She flipped through her bar clothes, smiling. Dresses with no back, dresses with very little front, dresses with huge full skirts and tiny waists; slinky things, sexy things, little-girl things; a cowgirl's outfit, something that looked like a nurse's uniform . . . She began to feel melancholy again and turned to the other closet, where her ordinary clothes hung.

She chose a sweater in almost exactly the same shade of blue as her eyes, and a flowered skirt that had some of the same color blue in it.

She put on the skirt and sweater and slipped her feet into a pair of dark-blue flat-heeled shoes.

She wore no underwear, and no jewelry.

Zoe scrunched up newspaper and laid kindling and then the two big pieces of wood on top. She got the matchbook out of her bathrobe pocket and lit the paper in three places. Then she scrabbled out from under the porch and ran.

She was halfway to the fence when she remembered the basket. She thought about leaving it there to burn up with the porch, but she knew her mother would miss it, so she turned around and ran back and grabbed it—just in time, too: it was warm, almost hot, when she touched it; the fire was already burning hard and making crackling noises.

Zoe sprinted across the old people's yard and threw herself over the fence and bolted for the back door of her house. Inside, she refilled the basket, put it back next to the fireplace and ran as quietly as she could upstairs to her room.

She sat looking out of her window while she caught her breath.

She watched as the old people's porch set fire to their house. It was a much bigger fire than she'd expected. She could smell the smoke and feel the heat from it all the way over here in her own yard, her own house, her own room.

She heard Benjamin come crashing up the stairs, yelling at the top of his lungs, and then her mother and father got up in a big hurry, shouting and banging doors.

Zoe got into bed and pulled the covers up to her chin.

The fire burned up the porch and the whole house and the old people, too, and Zoe's anger got burned up with them.

Zoe looked into the mirror and smoothed the palms of her hands over her face. She slowly ran her fingers through her hair, first one hand, then the other, five times each. She looked at herself critically and saw a serious face, with steady eyes. She watched herself, looking for signs of anger, or of fear, but there were none.

She went into the kitchen for two dishpans and a paring knife.

In the living room she put on the tape of Pachelbel's "Canon." She turned the sound up, switched off the lights, and returned to her bedroom.

She left the door open wide, to let the music in.

She lay in the middle of her bed, positioned the dishpans on either side of her, and cut her wrists with the paring knife.

When they found her the next day, practically all of the blood had fallen into the dishpans.

C H A P T E R

53

A watch was kept all night on Zoe Strachan's driveway.

The next afternoon, headquarters faxed to Alberg the report from the lab. It said that the scribblers appeared to have been written by Zoe Strachan.

He also received word from the fire inspector that arson was suspected in the blaze that had destroyed her cottage.

He told Sokolowski to follow in a patrol car, and he set off for Zoe Strachan's house.

By the time he got there, she had been dead for eighteen hours.

When he finally returned to the detachment at six o'clock, Isabella was still at her desk.

"Isabella. I told you to go home hours ago."

"I know," she said, cranking paper into her typewriter. "It's better that I keep busy."

He sat on the edge of her desk. "I'm sorry about Ramona."

"I know you are," she said. "You did all you could. She just didn't want us to find her."

"She saved the kid's life, you know."

"That's what I heard." She looked up at him. "You look awful. If you don't mind my saying so."

"I don't mind." He went down the hall to his office, pulling off his jacket. He sat behind his desk and rubbed his face with both hands. "Jesus, Jesus, Jesus," he muttered.

There was a knock at the door. "What is it?"

She opened the door. "Bernie Peters is here to see you. Right here behind me," she added quickly.

"No, Isabella," he said wearily. "Please. Send her away."

Isabella vanished, and a small, nut-brown person materialized in his doorway.

"Howdyedo," she said, sticking out her hand.

Her face looked like crunched-up tissue paper. He'd never seen so many lines and creases.

He floundered to his feet and shook her hand. "Karl Alberg."

"She says you're wanting somebody to do for you."

He was pretty sure her hair was dyed. It was an unnaturally brilliant shade of brown. She wore it in tiny curls, covered by a hairnet.

"Well, I was, yes . . ."

She wore a white uniform under a waist-length brown jacket. On her feet were white shoes, the kind worn by nurses and waitresses. From her bony wrist dangled a pea-green purse.

"Well, are you? Or ain't you?" She peered at him with bright eyes, small and black.

Alberg studied her for a moment, then sat down behind his desk. "I have to ask you some questions."

"Shoot."

"Have you got anything against unmarried men?"

"Nope."

"Or cats?"

"Nope."

"How about police officers?"

"Police officers saved my bacon more times than I can count."

"Really?" he said hopefully. "Sit down, sit down, Ms. Peters."

"I don't mind if I do."

"Good. Now. Go on."

"I was a married woman for a period of time."

"Uh huh."

"But I picked myself a bad apple."

Alberg gave a sympathetic cluck.

"He used to wallop me."

"Was this here? In Sechelt?"

"Nowhere else."

"Huh. How long did you stick it out?"

"Seventeen lickings he gave me, before we finally got him put away."

"Jesus."

"I don't hold with blasphemy."

"Sorry. Where is he now?"

"Nineteen seventy-five it was. He's out by now, of course. But he dispatched himself well away from here, you can bet your boots on that."

She sat with her back straight, her feet together, her green purse upright on her lap. He had absolutely no idea how old she was.

"Well. I do need some help, all right."

"I could come Wednesday afternoons or Monday mornings."

"How about Wednesday afternoons."

She stood up. "Done," she said. "I'll be there one o'clock on the dot through till five. She'll tell me how to get to your place, the typer out there." Again, she stuck out her hand. "I'm pleased to make your acquaintance," she said.

C H A P T E R

54

At the end of the day Alberg went home, and as he drove he thought about Kenny, now safely delivered to the house of his friend Roddy, to await the arrival of his grandparents. And he thought about Ramona, too.

And about Zoe Strachan, twice an arsonist. Responsible for three deaths. Probably four, if she'd shoved her brother down the stairs.

A late-winter rain had arrived during the afternoon, and it continued to fall, sometimes heavy, sometimes light, as Alberg drove. The wind had picked up, too, and he made his way more slowly than usual along the highway between Sechelt and Gibsons, watching for tree branches on the road. There was very little traffic on the highway.

It was dark when he got home. He'd forgotten to leave a light on in his house, and it looked dead, he thought, sitting there on the side of the hill: bleak, inert, unoccupied, and dead, a corpse of a house.

But it wasn't unoccupied, he reminded himself. And therefore it certainly wasn't dead.

He pulled up next to the somewhat rickety fence, upon which great masses of hydrangea bushes leaned, their uncut blooms now a brown-gold color, as though winter had rusted them. He walked up the cracked sidewalk to the front door, considering again whether he ought to try to purchase his house instead of continuing to rent it; or maybe he should start looking for something else to buy. This damn place was old and badly cared for; it was probably falling apart around him.

Ramona Orlitzki had been a hero; Alberg wondered if she'd known that, before she died.

Inside, he called for the gray cat and heard a squeaky meow in response. He turned on the hall light and saw her get up from the sofa in the living room, slowly, stretching first her front legs and then her back legs, yawning. He'd been very pleased when she and her kitten, who was now an adult cat, had first begun sleeping in the house instead of in the cardboard box in the sunporch. It was good to have other creatures living in the house with him. Neither of them had names; he called the older one Cat and the younger one Number Two. She was black, with white front paws and white on her chest and smeared across her mouth. She was curled up on a chair in his bedroom.

He fed the cats, talking to them as he did so, and he wondered if Zoe Strachan had liked animals. He looked into the blunt, triangular faces of his cats and thought that these creatures were more present, more substantive, than Zoe Strachan had been.

No, of course she hadn't liked animals. She hadn't liked people, either. He wondered what she *had* liked; there must have been something. . . .

He felt like calling his daughters. But today he didn't want to be distracted; he wanted to be understood.

He thought about calling Maura. But she was probably out with her damned accountant.

He turned off the lights and sat in his living room for a while, in the wingback chair by the window, with his feet up on the hassock. He left the curtains open and sat there quietly, watching the rain falling, and the wind shaking the hydrangea bushes.

Soon he didn't want to share his cheerless state with anyone, after all. It seemed appropriate to overload for a while on melancholy.

He heard a car, and Cassandra's Hornet appeared, and pulled up behind his Oldsmobile. Alberg swore softly under his breath. He watched, feeling surly, as she got out of her car and looked from his white Oldsmobile to the darkened house. He could tell that she wasn't sure what she should do. He began to feel guilty. But he didn't move to turn on a light. She hesitated beside her car, the driver's door still open. Then she slammed it shut and walked swiftly toward the house.

Alberg got out of his chair.

"Hi," he said, when he'd opened the door. Her hair had rain-sparkles all over it. Her cheeks were flushed.

"I've just taken my mother home," said Cassandra. "Bag and baggage. I've come to take you to Victoria."

Alberg felt a sudden prickling at the backs of his eyes. He shut them tight, and reached for her, and wrapped his arms around her. "What a hell of a good idea," he said.

FOR THE BEST IN MYSTERY, LOOK FOR THE

☐ A CRIMINAL COMEDY
Julian Symons

From Julian Symons, the master of crime fiction, this is "the best of his best" (*The New Yorker*). What starts as a nasty little scandal centering on two partners in a British travel agency escalates into smuggling and murder in Italy.
220 pages   ISBN: 0-14-009621-3   **$3.50**

☐ GOOD AND DEAD
Jane Langton

Something sinister is emptying the pews at the Old West Church, and parishioner Homer Kelly knows it isn't a loss of faith. When he investigates, Homer discovers that the ways of a small New England town can be just as mysterious as the ways of God.
256 pages   ISBN: 0-14-778217-1   **$3.95**

☐ THE SHORTEST WAY TO HADES
Sarah Caudwell

Five young barristers and a wealthy family with a five-million-pound estate find the stakes are raised when one member of the family meets a suspicious death.
208 pages   ISBN: 0-14-008488-6   **$3.50**

☐ RUMPOLE OF THE BAILEY
John Mortimer

The hero of John Mortimer's mysteries is Horace Rumpole, barrister at law, sixty-eight next birthday, with an unsurpassed knowledge of blood and typewriters, a penchant for quoting poetry, and a habit of referring to his judge as "the old darling."
208 pages   ISBN: 0-14-004670-4   **$3.95**

FOR THE BEST IN MYSTERY, LOOK FOR THE

☐ **MURDOCK FOR HIRE**
Robert Ray

When he is hired to find a dead man's missing antique coin collection, private detective Matt Murdock discovers an international crime ring that is much more than a nickle-and-dime operation.
256 pages   ISBN: 0-14-010679-0   **$3.95**

☐ **BRIARPATCH**
Ross Thomas

This Edgar Award-winning thriller is the story of Benjamin Dill, who returns to the Sunbelt city of his youth to attend his sister's funeral—and find her killer.
384 pages   ISBN: 0-14-010581-6   **$3.95**

☐ **DEATH'S SAVAGE PASSION**
Orania Papazoglou

Suspense is killing Romance, and the Romance Writers of America are outraged. When a fresh, enthusiastic creator of the loathed hybrid, Romantic Suspense, arrives on the scene, someone shows her just how murderous competition can be.
180 pages   ISBN: 0-14-009967-0   **$3.50**

☐ **GOLD BY GEMINI**
Jonathan Gash

Lovejoy, the antiques dealer whom the *Chicago Sun-Times* calls "one of the most likable rogues in mystery history," searches for Roman gold coins and greedy bird-killers on the Isle of Man.
224 pages   ISBN: 0-451-82185-8   **$3.95**

☐ **REILLY: ACE OF SPIES**
Robin Bruce Lockhart

This is the incredible true story of superspy Sidney Reilly, said to be the inspiration for James Bond. Robin Bruce Lockhart's book tells the thrilling story of the British Secret Service agent's shadowy Russian past and near-legendary exploits in espionage and in love.
192 pages   ISBN: 0-14-006895-3   **$4.95**

☐ **STRANGERS ON A TRAIN**
Patricia Highsmith

Almost against his will, Guy Haines is trapped in a nightmare of shared guilt when he agrees to kill the father of the man who will kill Guy's wife. The basis for the unforgettable Hitchcock thriller.
256 pages   ISBN: 0-14-003796-9   **$4.95**

☐ **THE THIN WOMAN**
Dorothy Cannell

An interior designer who is also a passionate eater, her rented companion who writes trashy novels, and a rich dead uncle with a conditional will are the principals in this delicious thriller.   242 pages   ISBN: 0-14-007947-5   **$3.95**